Praise for Nikk

"Gia makes me want to holler out loud—she knows how
to think for herself and she definitely has enough drama to fill
a thousand pages! I soooo loved Gia's voice. She's real, and I
know readers will love her, too!"
—Michelle Stimpson, author of *Trouble in My Way*

"*Step to This* is hot, it's new, it's now . . . with characters
that leap from the pages, it's absolutely a must-read."
—Monica McKayhan, *Essence* © bestselling author of
Indigo Summer

"*Step to This* is a wonderful, witty tale that is full of
laugh-out-loud moments and great lessons."
—Victoria Christopher Murray, author of
the Divine Divas series

"Nikki Carter is a fresh, new voice in teen fiction! *Step to This* has
it all—drama, humor, and a lesson that everyone can learn from. Full
of fun-loving, unforgettable characters that readers will love, Nikki
has written a page-turner that will leave the reader wanting more!"
—ReShonda Tate Billingsley, author of The Good Girlz series

"*Step to This* has alluring characters, wonderful scenes,
and a fascinating premise. Nikki Carter has
a real talent for writing stories that deal with real issues
but are gripping to read by teens and adults alike."
—Jacquelin Thomas, author of The Divine Series

"Filled with smart and witty characters, *Step to This* is a
fun, fast-paced read teens will love."
—Ni-Ni Simone, author of *A Girl Like Me*

"Nikki Carter steps up and delivers a home run with her
debut novel, *Step to This*. It's a real winner."
—Chandra Sparks Taylor, author of *Spin It Like That*
and *The Pledge*

Also by Nikki Carter

Step to This

Published by Kensington Publishing Corporation

it is what it is

A So For Real Novel

nikki carter

KENSINGTON PUBLISHING CORP.

www.kensingtonbooks.com

Acknowledgments

I would like to first thank God for making this whole writing thing possible! I am so excited to be able to share my stories with the world. It's a blessing and a privilege.

I'm also blessed to have a supportive husband, Brent. Thanks to my biggest fans, Briana, Brittany, Brynn, Brent II, and Brooke! I also want to thank all of the youth ministries and educators who have helped get the word out about the So For Real series.

Thank you to the entire team at Kensington, and to the best agent ever—Pattie Steele Perkins!

Many extra thanks to my editor, Mercedes, for being a treasure-trove of slanguage. Womp, womp!

Thanks to all of the music artists who helped me get my write on!

Thank you to all of my author mentors and friends who support, give blurbs, do shout-outs, and totally have my back! ReShonda, Yolonda, Bonnie, Victoria, and Norma—thank y'all!

And, finally, a great big shout to my readers! Keep it tight, and tell a friend. ☺

Holla!

Nikki

Are bridesmaid dresses supposed to itch?

I'm asking because my mom, Gwen, has me standing in front of the church wearing a ridiculous amount of pink taffeta and some other material that's making me itch. I close one eye and try to concentrate on making the itch disappear, because it's in the center of my back, right where I can't reach it.

The concentration isn't working, so I shift my shoulders in little circles trying to reach the itch with the zipper on my dress.

"Gia, will you *stop* it?" hisses my cousin, Hope. "Auntie Gwen is gonna get you when she sees you squirming on her wedding video."

She's right. Gwen will be heated. But it's her own fault. She shouldn't have picked outfits that make us look like Destiny's Child backup dancers. All of this shining and glistening is a bit extra if you ask me. The only good thing about this dress is that it amps up my miniature curves. Yes, I have officially gone from skinny to slim. You don't know the difference? Well, boo to you. The distance from skinny to slim is about the same as the distance from thick to plump. Marinate on it.

Even though I'm sixteen and on my way into the eleventh grade, this is Gwen's first wedding. She met a guy at our church named Elder LeRon Ferguson and they really hit it off. Even the pastor (who is also my uncle) was happy about them getting together. On the real, I think the only two people *not* happy about this whole blessed affair are me and Elder LeRon's daughter, Candy.

Don't get it twisted, I want my mother to be happy, get a man and all that, but I just thought it would all take place after I was grown. I am so not in the mood for a new daddy and a bratty little sister who will probably make my life miserable.

But if Gwen is going to be upset 'cause I'm trying to scratch my itch, then she's gonna be extra heated when she sees Candy on video. She practically stomped down the aisle and didn't even hold her flower bouquet up in front of her. She let her arms drop to her sides and mean-mugged the video guy all the way to the front of the church.

This itch is really starting to drive me nuts. This whole wedding ceremony thing is taking forever, too! Gwen had to go all out and have three flower girls and a miniature bride. I mean, for real, is all that even necessary?

As the third flower girl marches up the aisle throwing

flowers everywhere but on the floor in front of her, Hope leans forward and whispers, "There's Ricky."

We both smile at *my* best friend Ricardo. Umm . . . yeah . . . survey says no. Hope needs to pause all of that action immediately. She's been lightweight digging Ricky ever since Homecoming of last year. And that's only because he got upgraded to "hot" status by Longfellow High's resident vixen, Valerie. She's the captain of the Hi-Steppers dance squad and not exactly my favorite person.

Ricky smiles back at us and waves. Even though I'm standing in the front of the church, I can tell he's looking real fresh and real clean. My mom would say he looks dapper in his church suit and tie. But I ain't Gwen, and *dapper* is a word for those old movies.

I know what you're thinking, and the answer is no! Ricky is just my friend, not my *boyfriend*. Gwen is dead set against me dating until I'm in college. This is not an exaggeration either. I totally wish I was exaggerating.

Finally, Gwen starts marching up the center aisle of the church. It's about time! When the entire congregation turns to watch her, I take my bouquet and try to scratch my back with the little plastic holder thingy.

My mom looks real pretty, kinda like me but older. She's grinning from ear to ear as everyone takes pictures of her. Since her only close male family member is her brother—my uncle, Pastor Stokes—she decided to walk down the aisle alone.

When I asked if Pastor was going to give her away, these were her exact words: "I'm a grown woman, and I belong to God. I'm giving myself away."

Oh the bluntness.

I am glad when Gwen makes her way up the three little steps to stand in front of Pastor and next to Elder LeRon. She looks real fly in her off-the-shoulder bridal gown that Hope and I helped her pick out. Aunt Elena helped too, but she's my uncle's wife and Gwen isn't really feeling her all like that.

Pastor Stokes starts up with his standard wedding sermon. He's talking about love, forgiveness, and all kinds of stuff I don't need to worry about right now. My new stepsister, Candy, sighs loudly like she's bored out of her mind. But Gwen gives her some serious I-will-cut-you-if-you-mess-up-my-wedding-day side eye and she pulls herself together quickly.

After the vows are exchanged, and Elder LeRon kisses my mom, the ceremony ends, although we have to stand up here letting everyone in the church hug and kiss us. I am so not feeling that. I've got about fifty different shades of lipstick smeared on my face, and everyone's breath is not fresh. I mean, if you're gonna eat an onion and pickle sandwich you can at least respect the personal space perimeter or get yourself some extra-strength Altoids. For real.

Speaking of people who don't respect personal space, clammy-hands Kevin is standing in line with his grandparents. Kevin has been in love with me for like ever, and trust, it is completely against my will. And why did he just wink at me? Boy, bye!

"Here comes your boyfriend," teases Hope.

Candy overhears and scrunches up her nose. "That's your boyfriend? You have horrible taste."

"Kevin is not my boyfriend," I argue. "Hope is the one who went out on a date with him."

Hope pinches the back of my arm and frowns. She would love to forget her "date" with Kevin. It was really supposed to be my first date with Romeo, a football player at Longfellow High. But Hope was in straight hater mode and invited herself on my date. That's why she ended up chilling with Kevin for the evening. Let's just say that was not a fun outing for Hope.

Actually, though, even though Kevin is the opposite of everything fab, he is a whole lot better than Romeo. Months have gone by, but I'm still somewhat irritated about how Romeo played me. You don't just get over a boy taking you out on a date and leaving you stranded at the beach, just because you won't get freaky with him.

I know that Jesus would forgive him, but I'm still getting there, okay?

Kevin finally makes it through the line and hugs everyone, including me. "Gia, you look really pretty."

"Thank you, Kevin," I reply with a tight smile.

I almost said something smart, but I'm practicing accepting compliments graciously. And if I do say so myself, outside of this pink, frilly monstrosity, I do look kinda hot! My hair is especially fresh because Gwen gave me a two-stranded twist-out.

I see you giving me a blank stare, so let me explain. My mom washed my hair and then put cream and gel in and twisted it down my back until it dried. Then she untwisted it and let the waves hang down on one side and pinned it up in the back.

Yeah, reread that and take a mental picture. Just trust me, okay? It's fly.

Next in the line is Ricky. Hope reaches ahead of me and hugs *my* best friend. I think I need to keep saying that, because Hope doesn't seem to understand. She's trying my patience.

Then Ricky hugs me too. "Are we going skating after the reception?"

"You know it!" I reply and give my boy a high-five.

Hope frowns at me. "Do you think you could act like a lady for five minutes?"

I roll my eyes at Hope and ask Ricky, "Can you scratch my back?"

"Gia!" exclaims Hope.

Ricky and I crack up laughing because we know this irritates Hope. Hope and I have only recently renewed our BFF status. We went through some drama during our freshman and sophomore years, but we're cool now.

Even though we're friends again, we have very different ideas on what is fab and what isn't fab. Hope thinks that wearing designer clothes and making sure her lip gloss matches her purse is fly. The only matching I do is to make sure I have on two of the same socks. Outside of that, it's a free-for-all.

Finally, it's time to head over to the church social hall for the wedding reception. Gwen got Sister Benjamin, from the kitchen ministry at church, to cater, and I'm getting super hungry thinking about her fried chicken and sugar yams. I'm about to get my serious grub on.

Hope, Candy, and I sit at the wedding-party table waiting for our food to be brought by the servers. I'm in chill mode, but Candy is looking like a straight hater with her arms crossed and her face pulled into a haterific frown.

"What's wrong with you, Candy?" asks Hope.

Candy looks Hope up and down and says, "Mind ya' bidness."

"Ugh," replies Hope. "You would be cute if you weren't so evil."

"And you would be cute if . . . well, nah, that would never happen," says Candy.

Can I just say that I agree with Hope? Candy has long, thick hair that she wears in a braid down the back of her head. Her eyes are big and pretty too, and she's got smooth dark brown skin with not even one pimple.

But Hope is right. Candy is not just evil . . . she's super-duper evil.

I never thought I'd meet anyone as sarcastic as me, but Candy has got me beat for real. Anytime she opens her mouth an insult comes out of it. Even if you say something nice to her, she gives off nothing but negativity.

It's not a good look.

"I'm going skating with you," Candy says as if it's true.

"Um . . . no you're not," I reply.

She lets out an evil cackle. "Oh, yes I am. I already asked your mother and she said that you had to let me come."

What! We'll see about this. I march right on down to the other end of the table where the new Mrs. Ferguson is grinning and cheesing. Yeah, she can calm all of that down, because we need to have a conference.

I tap Gwen on the shoulder and she looks up. "Hi, sweetie. The food will be out in a minute."

"Okay, but did you tell Candy that she could go skating with me and Ricky?"

She pauses for a moment like she's trying to remember. Then she says, "Yes, I think I did. LeRon and I think you two should get to know each other, since you'll be living under the same roof."

"Mom, that's not fair. She's not even nice, and I don't want her around my friends." I know I'm whining, but I really am not feeling this.

Gwen frowns. "Too bad. She's your new sister and sisters stick together."

"But, Mom!"

"Deal with it, Gia!" Gwen fusses. "Don't make me get ugly with you on my wedding day. You are about to make me mess up my makeup."

Elder LeRon sits down next to my mother and asks, "Is everything all right, Gwennie? Gia, why are you frowning?"

Gwen gives me a look that says, *You better not say anything.*

So, I don't. I go back down to our end of the table and eat my food in silence. Not even Sister Benjamin's extra crispy chicken and sugary yams are making me feel better. And Candy isn't helping either, sitting there with a smirk on her face.

Candy leans over and whispers, "I told you, Gia. Your mother wants me to like her and she's going to do anything I ask. Me and you are going to have lots of fun this year."

Why do I get the feeling that her idea of fun is my idea of torture?

★ 2 ★

What in the hot-Ikea-mess is this silver monstrosity sitting in the middle of Candy's room? I think it's a bed, but the fabulousness in me won't allow me to sleep on it. And Gwen is grinning too hard! Ugh! Ever since she and her man got back from the Bahamas, she's been *extra*.

Let me backtrack, because I see you looking all confused.

Today is moving day for me and Gwen. Instead of my mother and her new husband getting a new spot, they decided to just move into LeRon's cramped, three-bedroom townhouse. It's cramped because now Candy is living here full-time. She used to visit LeRon just during the holidays and stuff after her parents divorced, but now her mom has a new boyfriend, and he is not ready for a kid, so her mom shipped her off to LeRon's.

Don't get it twisted, this place is a whole lot better than

that little shack that Gwen and I used to call home. But I have no intentions of sharing a bedroom or a metal bunk bed with the evilness that is Candy. Not even if they put a purple Tweety comforter on there, with purple furry Tweety pillows.

Side bar . . . the Tweety madness is hot, even if it is probably against man law for Tweety to be wrapped up in all that purple. You didn't know? Tweety is a boy! He is my boyfriend, by the way. He stays rocking that yellow bald head.

But anyway, enough about my man and back to the foolishness that is this sleeping arrangement.

"Mom," I ask, "didn't you say that this house has three bedrooms? Why do Candy and I have to share?"

LeRon answers, "Because the third bedroom is my study. It's where I prepare my sermons and pray."

And? Am I supposed to be cramped up just because he gets to teach Sunday school? And why does he get to make all the rules? I know my mom doesn't make much money as an LPN, but she is paying some bills up in this piece!

Gwen adds, "Sweetie, LeRon needs his study room and there is nothing wrong with two sisters sharing a room. I shared with your Aunt Penelope."

Yes, I know she shared with Auntie Penny. I also know that they fought like two crazy people while they were teenagers. They *still* fight! My uncle is always breaking them up at the family Christmas dinner.

As if Gwen is reading my mind she says, "Look, maybe me and Penny wasn't a good example. I think you and Candy are really going to get along."

Candy looks at me with a diabolical grin on her face. Yeah, I don't think so. Gwen gets a big, fat *No, ma'am!*

"I picked the top bunk, Gia, that's why all that Tweety stuff is on the bottom," Candy says, sounding all pumped like she just won some Rihanna tickets on the radio. Girl, boo.

I reply, "I don't care which bed you picked, because I am not sleeping in here."

Candy drops her head and looks at the floor, as if her feelings are hurt. And if I believed that Candy actually *has* feelings then maybe I'd be convinced.

"Where do you think you're sleeping then?" asks Gwen.

I don't have an answer to this question, of course. I haven't thought that far ahead in this scenario.

"I don't know," I say slowly. "Maybe on the couch in the living room."

Gwen puts one hand on her hip. "Try again, sweetheart."

"The basement?" I ask.

"Nope."

In a very, very small voice I take one last shot. "The garage?"

Gwen's hand drops from her hip, and for a second she looks sad too. Maybe someone should've asked me how I felt about all of this. I mean, nobody consulted me when my mom started dating Elder LeRon, nobody asked me about a wedding, and I definitely don't remember being asked about sleeping arrangements in this strange house.

My mom sighs and says, "Gia, this is not going to be easy for any of us. Candy has been used to having her own room, and you don't see her complaining."

Oh no, Candy is not standing up here with an angelic smile on her face. You've got to be kidding me. All three of them—Gwen, LeRon, and Candy—are looking at me like they're waiting for me to say something. So, I give them what they want.

"All right. I'll try it out for a minute, I guess."

Candy's eyes light up. Gwen smiles and says, "Thank you. I knew you would. We'll work something out, though, so you can have your own space. I promise."

"There's nothing to work out," says Elder LeRon.

Gwen raises one eyebrow and gives her husband a side-eye glance. "We can talk about this later, LeRon."

She gave him her *I don't play* voice, which I guess he already knows about, because he puts both hands in the air like he's done with this.

Gwen claps her hands together and says, "Well, girls, LeRon and I are going to watch these movies we rented. You two can get settled in and better acquainted."

LeRon interjects, "Do you think this is a good time to talk about the rules?"

Rules? Excuse me . . . what? I feel a fever coming on.

"Maybe we should let this bedroom situation sink in first," replies Gwen.

I plop down on the Tweety bed and say, "Mom, we might as well get this over with."

Candy nods in agreement, so Gwen shrugs her shoulders and says, "Go ahead, Ron. Tell them."

He smiles and clears his throat like he's about to give an acceptance speech on the BET awards. This whole afternoon is going from bad to worse.

Elder LeRon says, "Let me start by saying that I am

happy to have my new wife and my new daughter here in our home."

His new *daughter*? Hmm . . . I'm not sure if I'm feeling that yet. What am I supposed to call him? Daddy? Dad? Papa?

"But," he continues, "in order for us to live in harmony, Gwen and I sat down and came up with a few rules. The first rule is that there is a ten o'clock curfew for both of you."

My eyebrows shoot all the way up. "Ten o'clock? Mom, I'm sixteen, about to be seventeen! Why should I have the same curfew as a freshman?"

Gwen bites her bottom lip. "That leads us into the second rule. Anytime you go out, Candy must go with you. We believe that there is strength in numbers."

Candy jumps into the air and squeals. I can't do anything because I'm in a catatonic state of shock. I think my eyes are blinking, but I'm not sure.

Gwen says, "Calm down, Gia. It's not going to be that bad. Candy is almost the same age as you guys and you only hang out with Ricky and Hope anyway."

"What about Hi-Steppers? She can't go to Hi-Steppers stuff!" I argue.

Candy responds, "I'm trying out for Hi-Steppers."

Jesus, take me. Take me now!

"Mom!" This is me screaming like a banshee now.

LeRon says, "I think that's a great idea, Candy. Then you and your new sister can have something in common."

Since my only response is folding my arms and frowning, LeRon continues. "There will be no phone calls from boys, or dates. We don't want any pregnant teenagers in this house. You'll have plenty of time to date when you're grown."

"What about Ricky?" I ask, not expecting Elder LeRon to say anything reasonable.

"No phone calls from him either. You can see Ricardo at school and church."

"LeRon, Ricky and Gia have been best friends for years. I think that's too much," says Gwen.

Well, finally she got my back. While she's back there maybe she can wipe off the tire tracks from the bus she threw me under.

LeRon frowns deeply. "I don't know, Gwen. We'll have some more discussion about this. Remember what happened last year."

Okay, so am I going to answer for one little mistake for the rest of my life? Yes, I snuck out on a date with Romeo. Yes, I lied. And yes, I got left standing at the beach looking right foolish. That was *sooooo* last year! Can we get beyond this?

"Well, I know Ricky's family and I know him. I am not concerned with him doing anything like that child Romeo," says Gwen.

Elder LeRon takes a long pause like he's thinking. "Well, all right. Ricky and Ricky only. If you break that rule, there will be a severe punishment."

Severe punishment? Okay, he must not know Gwen very well if he thinks he's scaring me with that. Severe punishment is her middle name. I think she invented severe punishment and used me as the test dummy.

Yeah, I'm not afraid of him. Plus, I've seen him get punked by Candy.

Gwen asks, "Gia, do you have a problem with this?"

"No. Is someone going to ask Candy if she has a problem with it?" I ask with much attitude. "Did you all just sit down and write these rules for me or are they for both of us?"

Trust and believe, I know I'm getting out of pocket. But Elder LeRon and Gwen are out of control here. I haven't heard one thing that's going to change Little Miss Evil's life.

"Honestly, Gia, we want to make sure that your past behavior doesn't wear off on Candy. She's at a very impressionable age right now," LeRon says.

Oh no he didn't! He better hope I wear off on that problem child. I get straight A's, and the *only* issue I've ever had was that one time with Romeo.

I take a slow, deep breath, because there's a chance that after I give my reply, I might not take another one.

"It sounds like you are judging me by my lowest point. I wonder if you would like it if Jesus judged you by your lowest point?"

Gwen frowns deeply. "Gia, I think you've lost your mind. Do you realize you're speaking with an adult?"

"I'm just repeating what I heard Bishop T. D. Jakes say on his broadcast. Does *Elder* LeRon have a problem with Bishop Jakes?"

Gwen closes her eyes and places her hand over her heart. I know this pose. This is when she's praying for strength not to do bodily harm to me. I haven't seen it in a while, but I do know it when I see it.

LeRon says, "Gia, I think you just need to get out of

your mother's sight for a while. We'll finish this discussion later."

"Well . . . you two are in my . . . our room."

Gwen replies through clenched teeth, "Girl, you better be glad I'm saved, sanctified, and filled with the Holy Ghost. I'm gon' deal with you later."

She walks out of the room muttering like a crazy person. LeRon follows her but glares over his shoulder at me. Whatev. They've got me messed up if they think this little Brady Bunch scenario is going to turn my life upside down.

Candy rushes to close the door behind them and then lets out a flurry of giggles. "You know you're going to pay for that, right?"

"Whatever. I don't care."

Why should I? With a ten o'clock curfew and an evil little stepsister tagging along, they've pretty much wrecked my life anyway.

★ 3 ★

"**R**icky, your new ride is fresh!"

Ricky beams a proud smile as he stands next to his new car. His mom helped him get a nineteen-ninety-something Pontiac Grand Am. It's blue with a silver interior and except for a few little rust patches, it looks great.

"Thanks, Gia. I knew you would like it."

Hope and Candy follow me out of the house so that we can all pile into Ricky's car and go school-clothes shopping. Hope was invited, but Little Miss Unsunshine was not. Unfortunately, we don't have a choice.

Hope narrows her eyes and grins at Ricky. I hope that's not supposed to be her seductive pose. If it is . . . then I vote no.

Plus, she just looks like she's squinting from the sun. It's hot, sunny, and sticky out here today, but by the first day of school, it'll be rainy season. That's something about the beginning of the school year here in Cleveland. Maybe it's the elements trying to insist on my hair looking like a beehive on the first day of school.

"Now that you have a car, you should come scoop me sometimes," says Hope in a kinda flirtatious tone.

Ricky laughs. "What do you think I'm doing now, silly?"

"I don't mean scoop me to go shopping . . . I mean . . . oh, never mind."

Hope can't seem to hide her frustration as she climbs into the backseat of Ricky's car. She must not realize that the boy she's trying to hook up with is utterly clueless. I guarantee that Ricky has no idea that she's trying to holla.

I'm still tripping at Ricky's random use of the word *silly*. Um . . . what?

"Get in the car, *silly*," I say to Ricky. "I'd like to get to the mall today."

Ricky clears his throat and replies, "You know I don't say *silly* all like that."

"Yes, you do," I say as I jump into my shotgun position.

As Ricky pulls off, he asks Candy, "This is a big year for you, right? Freshman year!"

"I guess it's cool. It probably won't be too different from middle school," replies Candy.

Okay, who isn't excited to start high school? There is something weird about this girl, for real. Methinks she's a clone.

Hope asks, "You aren't just a little bit excited?"

I yawn loudly and look out of the window. Candy is so transparent to me. She's only acting like she isn't excited so that she'll get Hope and Ricky's attention while they try to convince her to be excited.

Boo . . .

"She is too excited," I say, bursting her bubble. "I heard her on the phone with her little friends talking about the matching outfits they plan to wear for the first day."

Hope scrunches up her nose. "Matching outfits? That's definitely not the business, Candy. You've got to be unique and make your own fashion statement."

Ricky and I glance at one another and burst out laughing. I know Hope is not talking about being unique. She and her crew have almost the exact same wardrobes in different colors. They have so many similar outfits, that they come to school dressed alike by accident!

"Whatever, Gia! You and that Tweety apparel is so ten years ago, and Ricky, don't you still wear Wranglers with the crease down the middle?"

I'm proud of Hope! She's been hanging with me long enough to get a little gusto about herself. She's got comebacks and everything.

Candy is finding all of this friendly conversation funny. "I thought you guys were best friends," she says.

"We are," Ricky replies. "We're just playing. Right, Hope?"

Hope smiles. "Of course. Gia, Tweety is banging."

"And Hope, your Juicy T-shirts in every color of the rainbow are most definitely the bidness," I say, returning Hope's smile.

"Well, I won't be rocking much Juicy. That's last year," says Hope. "Junior year is gonna be all about Dolce, Lucky, and Prada."

Candy's eyes get wide. "Wow. Your mom lets you buy all those designers?"

"Yeah, she gives me my dad's credit card and just tells me not to get too crazy."

"Must be nice," says Candy with a frown.

Hope being a spoiled brat is no surprise to me and Ricky. We've known this about her since we were in kindergarten. My uncle, Pastor Stokes, is a great church leader, but if he has a weakness, it's his little girl. She has him completely trained.

As for my own personal fashion statement, I plan to give Mr. Tweety a rest this year. It's junior year, and time for something new, I think. I'm going vintage, like lace, pearls, black jeans, and red shoes. Kinda like Beyoncé's little sister, Solange. Don't you just love her? She's so *anti*.

We pull into the mall parking lot and Ricky circles several times looking for the perfect parking spot. I'm too ready to get out of the car because this money that I made working for Mother Cranford is burning a hole in my pocket and I'm ready to spend it.

I should say the money I made *slaving* for Mother Cranford. She's a mother at our church and the only employer I'm allowed to have. I think she created dust bunnies for me to vacuum. And when I cleaned out the garage, I'm so serious, there were newspapers in there from the Boston Tea Party.

"Good grief, Ricky! Would you just park!" I exclaim as we circle the lot for the fifth time.

"What? It's hot out here!"

Hope chimes in. "Right. Drop me off at the front, Ricky, because I'm not trying to go in the mall all sweaty and glistening."

What a diva! And what's wrong with Ricky? Boys aren't supposed to mind sweating.

Candy says, "I bet you get hot enough on the football field, right, Ricky?"

What in the out-of-the-blue? Okay, I'm not sure if Candy is trying to flirt, but from the look of Hope's mean mug, it is definitely not welcome.

"I do sweat a lot on the field, Candy. We're doing two-a-days now, too! Gia, did I tell you Coach Rogers is gonna start me this year?" says Ricky all nonchalantly as he finally pulls into a parking space.

"No! You didn't tell me that!" I give Ricky a high-five.

"Juniors taking over up in HEERRE!" says Hope with a shout.

My boy is the starting quarterback and I'm going to be rocking those little white Hi-Stepper boots on the field during the halftime show! This year is gonna be too for real.

As we walk across the parking lot, Candy asks, "So, Hope, what do you do? I know Gia is a Hi-Stepper and Ricky plays football. Are you a cheerleader?"

"Uh, no!" says Hope indignantly. "I signed up to be a rally girl."

"What's a rally girl?"

I smile to myself. The answer to that question all depends on who you ask. The football team thinks that the rally girls are their personal slaves who they can force to do their homework and tutor them when they're about to fail a class. The cheerleaders think that the rally girls are wannabes who couldn't cut it in the cheer universe.

The Hi-Steppers don't even acknowledge the rally girls' existence except when they are throwing a particularly fresh party.

But the rally girls think they're the hottest things walking. They plan all of the pep rallies and after parties. Like the Homecoming dance and then the Homecoming after party. But it looks like I won't be attending any after parties—not if they take place *after* ten.

Hope answers Candy. "The rally girls are all about bringing school spirit! Not just for football either, for every sport."

Yes, that is true. The rally girls don't discriminate. They party all school year long.

"Okay, enough about this! I didn't come to the mall to define the rally girls. I came to get my shop on," I say matter-of-factly.

We start off in one of Hope's favorite stores—Macy's. Ricky leaves us and heads off to the men's section while we tear through the racks in the juniors section. There is only one item that I need from here—skinny jeans.

Hope holds up a black Dolce & Gabbana T-shirt and asks, "What do y'all think?"

"That's hot!" exclaims Candy, sounding like a chocolate Paris Hilton.

It's not really my cup of tea, so I just give a shrug and a smile. "If you like it, I love it!"

Hope looks at it again, frowns, and then puts it back down. She says, "I'm one thousand percent sure that both Jewel and Kelani already have this."

"You think? They like their stuff a little bit more bedazzled, and there is not one rhinestone on that T-shirt." I say, thinking mostly of the blinding outfits that Jewel and Kelani like to wear.

Hope laughs. "You're probably right. This is something more Valerie's speed."

"Do y'all mean Valerie Lopez, the captain of the Hi-Steppers?" Candy asks.

Can somebody say thirsty? Why does she already know the first and last name of the Hi-Steppers' captain? If she makes the squad, and that's a big *if,* Valerie will probably put her on the B squad simply because she's a freshman.

"Yes, that's the Valerie we mean," I say.

"She's so cool!" gushes Candy. "She dated one of my friend's brothers and she treated us just like her little sisters. I can't wait to be a Hi-Stepper!"

Thirsty much?

★ 4 ★

Today is the first day of Hi-Steppers camp. It is two weeks before school starts and it's when we perfect our beginning-of-the-year routines. It's also when we pick a team captain, if necessary. Since Valerie was a junior last year, it's pretty much a given that she's gonna continue to be the captain for her senior year.

I step onto the football field where Mrs. Vaughn, our teacher advisor, is standing in her all-white workout gear. She's got her favorite accessory, her whistle, hanging around her neck.

Jewel and Kelani, who are already here and dressed in matching Baby Phat shorts and tees, run up to me and give me a hug. It's hilarious how cool we are now. Last year I was almost like an outcast to them, because I didn't dress like them or wear my hair like them. Actually, the only reason Valerie wanted me on the squad was to get at Ricky.

Yeah, that backfired on her and so did a horrible Gia-makeover. But that was last year and I've totally forgiven Valerie. I'm cool with Kelani and Jewel, even though we aren't BFFs (that's not *ever* going to happen).

Jewel asks, "Is Hope coming with you?"

I roll my eyes and frown. Jewel already knows what it is. After Hope got bumped down from the A squad to the B squad for messing up a routine, she was not feeling the Hi-Steppers anymore. Especially after the foul way that Valerie bumped her. It was not pretty.

Kelani answers for me. "I thought I told you! Hope is gonna be a rally girl."

"A what? Ewww!" Jewel scrunches her face so tightly that you can barely see her little blue eyes.

"Come on, Jewel. If you were Hope, would you want to be a Hi-Stepper?" I ask.

I didn't notice Valerie walk up to our conversation, but she answers my question. "Why wouldn't anyone want to be a Hi-Stepper?"

Jewel and Kelani look at each other as if they're deciding to let Valerie in on the rest of the conversation. They are so lame and still afraid of Valerie. I pity them.

I look Valerie up and down. Nothing has changed in the looks department. Valerie is still hot to death. She's got her hair pulled up into a ponytail and has on a tiny tank and some biker shorts. I wish I had even a fraction of those curves. As a matter of fact, I prayed all summer for those curves. Apparently the Lord did not hear my plea.

I reply, "Hope wouldn't want to be a Hi-Stepper, not even if you paid her."

"Oh, her!" exclaims Valerie with a laugh. "We wouldn't pay her either! That chica can't step to save her life."

I grin and shake my head. Valerie stays trying to integrate Spanish into her vocab. She knows good and well that even though she's Latina she ain't nowhere near bilingual.

But she is right. Hope was barely functional as a Hi-Stepper. She only got on the squad by kissing lots of Hi-Stepper bootay. That got old really, really quick. Plus, it's hard to kiss someone's bootay when they're totally dogging you out.

Mrs. Vaughn interrupts our conversation by blowing her whistle. Then she gives the Hi-Stepper call. "Ooo-OOO!"

"Ooo-OOO!" chirp all the Hi-Steppers in response.

Mrs. Vaughn says, "This year we are going to rock some hot new routines! But first, I need to whip your butts into shape, because it looks like you've been chilling all summer long!"

Everyone groans at once, because we know what this means.

"Give me one hundred jumping jacks! And ONE!" shouts Mrs. Vaughn.

After half killing us with one hundred jumping jacks, seventy-five squats, and three laps around the field, Mrs. Vaughn lets us have a two-minute water break. First of all, she's tripping! It's not like we have to play an entire game like the football players. We're on the field for six minutes tops, and then we're only doing cute dance moves. Second of all . . . well, I don't need a second of all! She's tripping!

After our two-minute break is up, Mrs. Vaughn tells us to line up in Hi-Stepper dance formation. Some of last year's squad has graduated, so we just kind of fill in where people are missing. Valerie and I end up standing next to one another, front and center.

"Now, let's see what you all remember from last year," says Mrs. Vaughn as she presses Play on her CD player.

"Oh" by Ciara blasts from the speakers and I immediately get into the groove. Not only is this one of my favorite songs, but the step was super-duper fly. And I remember tutoring half of the Hi-Stepper squad until they got it right. Actually, this is the step that got Hope exiled from the Hi-Steppers.

Of course, I'm doing the step flawlessly and even better than Valerie, who misses a turn and the cue for the hip-swivel rock. She's not as bad as everyone else though, who totally turned into vegetables over the summer.

Mrs. Vaughn cuts the music halfway through the song. "You all look pitiful. Everyone but Valerie and Gia, have a seat."

Valerie gives me some mean side eye and goes back to the starting position. I do the same. What's going on? Is this some kind of dance-off?

Bring it!

Mrs. Vaughn restarts the song and we start the step again. This time, Valerie's memory is better and she's just as flawless as I am. But she can't handle this, because not only do I have the step down perfectly, I've got the ad-libs. I bust a sweet crossover turn and go right back into the choreography. All the Hi-Steppers cheer, except Valerie of course. Even Mrs. Vaughn claps her hands.

This time when Mrs. Vaughn turns off the music, she tells everyone else to stand up. Then she says, "It looks like this year, we're going to have co-captains."

Was that what that was all about? Were we dancing off to decide captains? Wow!

Valerie folds her arms and frowns. "I've worked hard for this, Mrs. Vaughn. I deserve to be captain all by myself! And I'm a senior."

"You're right, Valerie. You have worked hard. That's why I'm not letting Gia be the sole captain. But I think that last year she showed her choreography skill and a lot of character."

By character, I'm sure Mrs. Vaughn means that whole Romeo scenario. I guess it did take some guts to even come back to school after Romeo left me stranded at the lake and then tried to make everybody think I was loose. I actually surprised myself.

Valerie takes my hand in her own and shakes it—hard. "Congratulations, Gia. I'm glad we're going to be co-captains."

I lift my eyebrows in shock. Valerie actually sounds sincere. Maybe she should try to get her mama to take her to Hollywood on some auditions, 'cause I'm ninety-nine point nine percent sure she's acting. Maybe she could be a Latina Hannah Montana or something.

I reply, "I'm happy too, Valerie. This is going to be a fun year."

Mrs. Vaughn dismisses the practice, and everyone comes up to congratulate me. Valerie hangs back, watching from a distance, with an evil expression on her face. I *knew* she wasn't feeling this co-captain stuff.

"You get to help pick out the newbies!" gushes Jewel. "My cousin is a freshman and she's trying out. She *really* wants to be a Hi-Stepper."

A queasy feeling takes over the pit of my stomach. I don't want to help pick out the new Hi-Steppers, especially not if Candy is going to try out.

Valerie finally breaks up the little congratulations party. "All right, everybody needs to get on home. We've got practice tomorrow morning, so get your rest."

I start to walk home with Jewel and Kelani, but Valerie grabs my arm. "Why don't you let me give you a ride, co-captain?"

"Um . . . okay."

Before I open the door to Valerie's car I check for booby traps. You think I'm playing, but I'm dead serious. Valerie is acting like she's got a case of the body snatchers going on. I cannot and will not be a statistic.

"Get in the car, chica!" exclaims Valerie. "What's your problem?"

"You first."

Valerie tosses her head back and lets out a loud cackle that I guess is supposed to be a laugh. Whatever.

When I'm finally sure it's safe, I get in and close the door. Valerie is still laughing at me as she starts the car.

"So what did you do all summer besides practice Hi-Stepper routines?" she asks.

"I didn't need to practice."

Valerie sucks her teeth and rolls her eyes. "Don't start getting cocky. You got out on me this once, but it'll never happen again."

"I wasn't trying to get out on you."

"Whatever. What's Rick been up to?"

Now I'm laughing. "Why do you care?"

"You know why."

"No, I really don't."

"Rick is starting QB this year. He has earned another opportunity to be my boyfriend."

My laughs have changed to snorts. And I'm almost choking. This girl is completely and totally unreal.

Valerie looks irritated. "Are you done?"

I take a deep breath, then another. I open up my mouth to answer her, but another flurry of laughter escapes.

"Okay," I reply, "now I'm done."

"What is so funny?"

I think back to how badly she played Ricky last year. She was kicking it with some college dude and Brad, who was a senior last year. Ricky was extra salty when he found out.

"Valerie, you had your chance with Ricky and you blew that. You had him open last year, but he's so over you."

"Is he dating someone new?" she asks.

"If he was, I wouldn't tell you."

"Why not?" she asks with attitude. "Hi-Steppers stick together!"

Oh no. She's not gonna pull that *Hi-Steppers stick together* mess on me. She forgot all about that last year when she helped Romeo play me like a dummy.

"Quit playing, Valerie. I mean, seriously."

Valerie sighs. "Listen, Gia, I know that we had some issues last year."

"That's an understatement."

"But I've been doing some personal reflection over the summer and I'm trying to be a better person."

Personal reflection? Wow. That's like a tiger deciding to be a vegetarian. Yeah, I don't believe her. Would you, if you were me?

"I'm serious, Gia! I don't like the way things ended with me and Rick. I'm so sorry for how I did him." No, she is not coming with the crocodile tears.

Against my own better judgment I say, "Have you told him that?"

"That's where I need your help, Gia. He won't talk to me."

"Ya think?"

"Seriously, I want to apologize to him."

Okay, maybe Valerie is a better actress than I give her credit for, because I actually kind of believe her. She really looks sad.

"I believe you, but it's not really about what I think. That's up to Ricky."

"I know, Gia! I'm not asking you to hook us up or anything like that. If you could just get him to talk to me . . ."

"Then what?"

She smiles. "Then I'll handle the rest."

I pause for a moment of my own personal reflection. If

I talk to Ricky for Valerie, I might have an easier time this year with the Hi-Steppers. I do not want Valerie for an enemy—that is just way too much unnecessary drama.

"Okay, Valerie, I'll see what I can do. But I'm not making any promises."

★ 5 ★

It's the night before the first day of school and Hope has insisted on spending the night at our house. It's funny—before Gwen and I moved in with LeRon and Candy, Hope never wanted to sleep over. I can't blame her, though. Our old crib was not exactly four-star accommodations.

"Hope, I do not need you to pick out my outfit. I already know what I'm wearing."

Hope narrows her eyes doubtfully. "That's like letting Mother Brown decorate your house."

"Mother Brown is blind."

Hope laughs. "Exactly!"

"I didn't know the pastor's daughter was allowed to clown the Mother's board."

Gwen pops her head into the bedroom. "Who on the Mother's board are you two talking about?"

"Nobody, Auntie Gwen."

Gwen clearly does not believe us. "Mmm-hmm. You two better be nice, because Jesus can hear you."

"We know, Mom!"

"Don't get smart with me, Gia! And where is Candy?"

I give Gwen a blank stare. "I didn't know I was supposed to be watching her."

"You're not supposed to be *watching* her. You should be trying to get to know your new sister."

Hope sighs and rolls her eyes. I feel the same way, but I have to live with Gwen. If I start rolling my eyes I might end up like Mother Brown. Ya feel me?

"Auntie Gwen, Candy is a freshman and we are juniors."

"And? I don't want you two leaving her out," Gwen replies. She's wearing her all-business face, which means it is not up for discussion.

"Candy!" Gwen calls. "Come on in here, girl."

Candy appears, holding a plate of leftovers from the dinner we just ate two hours ago and a glass of grape Kool-Aid.

"Yes, Gwen?"

Gwen strokes the back of Candy's head. "I just wanted you to be in on all the fun."

"They don't have to hang out with me if they don't want to," replies Candy with a juvenile pout.

"Yes, they do. Gia is your sister and Hope is now your cousin."

Candy continues in her fake, they're-being-mean-to-me voice. "It's okay. I don't want to be a burden. I'll just go and read some encyclopedias."

More blank stares at Gwen. She can't possibly be falling

for this mess. She's not even D-list good. She's like Solange in that made-for-television sequel to *Bring It On* (I love me some Sol-angel, but you know what I mean).

"Ma, I got this. Why don't you go tend to your new husband."

Gwen lifts her eyebrows. "You betta watch yourself."

Gwen sashays out of our bedroom like she just invented world peace. Once she closes the door behind her, Candy starts giggling.

"Your mom is so easy, Gia. We are going to get along great!"

"Auntie Gwen don't play, Candy."

Candy dismisses Hope by waving her hand in the air. She narrows her eyes and checks out my outfit that I've laid out on the bed. It's a pair of black skinny jeans, a gray baby tee, and a black vest. I bought a pile of Dollar Store beads that I'll be wearing around my neck too. With my funky afro and hoop earrings, that's going to be straight hotness indeed.

"That's all no-name stuff," Candy says.

"Wearing a brand name across your chest is so 2004. I like it, Gia," says Hope.

Candy goes to her drawer and pulls out a T-shirt. "This is what I'm wearing tomorrow."

My jaw is hanging open like a broken screen door. It's the Dolce & Gabbana T-shirt from the department store. Number one, I know Candy did not buy that when we went shopping, and number two, she didn't have the money even if she wanted it.

"Where'd you get that?" asked Hope. "Did you buy that when we went school shopping?"

"Yeah. I got it when we went to the mall."

Oh, she thinks somebody is stupid. "You *got* it when we were at the mall. With what money? That shirt was sixty dollars."

Candy holds her finger up to her mouth. "Will you be quiet?"

"Why I gotta be quiet?" I say . . . louder.

"Because I don't want your mom coming in here."

Hope asks, "Did you steal that T-shirt?"

"*Steal* is such an ugly word," says Candy.

What in the world? Candy's got sticky fingers. That's kind of ironic, because when you eat candy you get sticky fingers . . . Get it? Whatever! Don't you womp, womp me.

But seriously, Candy stole something while she was shopping with me. That is so not cool. And LeRon thinks I'll be a bad influence on her? Anyway!

"Isn't your dad gonna wonder how you came home with a designer T-shirt?" I ask. I need to hear if she's thought this thing all the way through, because I'm not trying to get in trouble with her.

"He doesn't know the difference between designer clothes and stuff you get at Target. My dad's clueless when it comes to this stuff."

"Well, Gwen isn't clueless," I respond. "So what do you plan to do about her if she asks?"

"I'll say I borrowed it from my rich friend Hope," says Candy with a wink.

As much as I hate to admit it, that would totally work on Gwen. She'd probably go into a rant on how spoiled Hope is and how she hopes her tithe and offering isn't being spent on the pastor's wife. Yeah, even though Pastor Stokes is her brother, she would totally go there.

Hope gets serious and says, "Candy, you know you don't have to steal designer stuff to be cool. Actually, stealing is the opposite of cool."

Candy looks like she's about to concur for a second, but then she bursts into laughter. "You are so funny! Do I look like an after-school special?"

"I'm telling my mom," I say angrily. Someone has to bring this child back to reality.

"Listen. Chill! I won't do it again. I just wanted something fresh to rock on the first day of school. I'll go up to the altar on Sunday and repent of my evils."

Hope looks satisfied, but I don't know if I believe Candy. I hope she pulls herself together, because a sista like me is not above snitching. I see you giving me the side eye, but if you had Ninja Gwen for a mother you'd snitch faster than a dope boy facing twenty years.

"So, Gia, can I ask you to do me a big, big favor?" asks Hope. I guess the subject has been officially changed.

"That depends on what it is."

Hope smiles and sits down on my bed. "Have I told you how much I'm glad to have you for a cousin and best friend?"

"What, Hope? What do you want?" I ask suspiciously.

"Well . . . do you know if Ricky has a girlfriend?"

I close my eyes and shake my head. I don't believe this. I honestly never thought that Hope would take it there, but here she is, and here it comes . . .

"And if he doesn't, do you think you could hook me

up?" she asks with this ridiculously angelic smile on her face.

"You like Ricky?" asks Candy.

"He has a ridiculous amount of hotness going on," gushes Hope. "Plus he's so sweet."

I'm still speechless. I should've seen this coming though. All of the hints she's been dropping to Ricky makes her beyond obvious. But Ricky? We've known him since we were babies.

Finally, I reply. "I think it's a conflict of interest for me to hook you up with Ricky. You're both my best friends."

"That should make it easier, right?" asks Candy.

"Wrong! What if they get together and then they break up?" I explain. "That would be all bad. That would completely mess up my friendship triangle."

Hope rolls her eyes. "Why would we break up? It's not like Ricky would play me, and I *definitely* won't be playing him."

"Stranger things have happened. If you want to get with Ricky, you're on your own, boo."

Hope frowns. "I can't stand you, Gia."

"I love you too, Hope."

★ **6** ★

"**G**ia, you look like a grown-up lady."
Why did I walk into the school, trying to make the main hallway the runway for my new no-Tweety look? Hope was on one side of me and Candy on the other as we walked to our lockers. I thought I was bringing it! Unfortunately, the only person who noticed all the fabulosity that is moi, was the ripeness that is Kevin.

He repeats his statement. "Did you hear me, Gia? I said you look like a grown-up lady."

I guess this is a compliment, so I say, "Thank you, Kevin. You look nice too."

Forgive me, Lord, for that small fib. Kevin doesn't exactly look *nice*. He looks almost normal with some faded jeans and a white T-shirt. It would look nice if he wasn't rocking it with his grandfather's dress belt and his shiny,

black patent leather church shoes. And why can't he just
Noxema his mocha-colored skin, and ask his grandmother
to take him to the barber? All those wild curls could be
waves. Even with a little acne he'd be kinda cute. What?
I'm just saying.

But did I mention that the T-shirt is tucked in? All the
way in. Where are those dudes from *What Not to Wear*
when you need them?

But speaking of fresh and clean, here comes Ricky walking down the hall. He waves at our little informal posse
and doesn't even seem to notice the girls who are giving
him double takes.

This year he's sporting a low haircut and it goes perfect
with his thick eyebrows and pretty eyes. His outfit is the
bidness too. His perfectly baggy jeans and a button-down
shirt are a fresh mix of nerd and jock. I vote yes!

"Hi, Ricky!" says Hope.

Ricky gives Hope a hug. "Hey, Hope! Happy first day
of school."

I make gagging noises. Ricky sure knows how to mess
up a flawless entrance. Happy first day of school? You
gotta be kidding me.

"What, Gia?" asks Ricky.

"Nothing, dude. I like your outfit. It's fresh."

"I like yours too," he replies, as I do a little turn so he
can get the full effect.

"Doesn't she look pretty?" asks Kevin.

Forgive me, Lord, for just rolling my eyes at my opposite-
of-secret admirer. I'm gonna need Kevin to simmer down.
It's too early in the morning for me to have to say all

these prayers of repentance. I get it. He likes me. But still . . . Boo!

Candy sees her freshman crew and says, "Holla! My girls are here."

Candy obviously chose to go against our advice, because she and her two best friends are wearing the exact same T-shirts in different colors. I wonder if they all got them with the five-finger discount.

"Thank goodness, her little friends are here! She is so irking!" I say.

Hope laughs. "Gia is a big sister. Wow!"

"I know, right! You've got to prepare somebody for this kind of invasion."

Ricky smiles. "I think she's sweet."

"She's sweet and sour," I reply truthfully.

Down the hall, I see Valerie and a group of other Hi-Steppers standing near the cafeteria. I guess Ricky sees her too, because now he's got a harsh frown on his caramel-colored face.

"What's the matter, Ricky?" asks Hope. She has strategically placed her hand on his back and is rubbing in little circles. So obviously, she's serious about this whole I-like-Ricky thing.

Ricky shakes his head. "Nothing. I'm good. Kev, let's roll out! We've got gym first period."

Hope's eyes follow Ricky as he and Kevin head toward the gymnasium. "He looks impossibly cute today."

"Eww!"

"What?" asks Hope innocently.

I cannot and will not tolerate this level of foolishness from Hope for the entire school year. I hope she gets over this Ricky thing quick, fast, and in a hurry. It is not a good look.

"Here comes *your* friend," Hope says as Valerie prances toward us.

"Ooo-OOO!" says Valerie. This is the Hi-Stepper greeting.

I give Valerie a high-five and shout, "Ooo-OOO!"

Hope says, "Hello, Valerie."

"The rally girl hopeful," Valerie says with a sneer. "Hello, Hope."

"That's right. I plan on becoming a rally girl, and I'm proud of it!"

Valerie laughs. "What is it that rally girls *do* again?"

"We are the spirit ambassadors of the school," Hope declares.

"We? Wow, you're pretty sure you'll make the squad, huh?" Valerie asks. "You never know what's going to happen."

Hope narrows her eyes and says, "Gia, I'll see you at lunch."

"Bye, Hope!" Valerie says as Hope storms away angrily.

Valerie leans against my locker and smiles at me. "So, have you talked to Ricky yet?"

"See, it's kind of complicated."

"Well, what are you waiting for?" she asks.

"I guess the right time hasn't come up."

"Well, I'm waiting, Gia. Don't let me down! I need to start picking out our Homecoming outfits."

Well, no one can say that she's not confident. Trouble is, this whole thing feels like . . . well . . . trouble. Especially since Hope has kicked her crush into overdrive. I don't think our newly mended friendship can make it through any kind of betrayal. This sounds like drama getting ready to happen.

And it's just the first day of school.

★ 7 ★

Candy looks nervous. Even though she's smiling from ear to ear and standing at attention, she looks ridiculously nervous. And she should. She's trying out for the Hi-Steppers.

It's rare for a freshman to make the squad at all, much less the A squad. Last year, I had the most flawless tryout ever and at first I only made the B squad. Valerie gave the foolish excuse that my image was not up to par.

Um . . . yeah. No.

When Candy's music starts, she begins her complicated routine. And, oh my goodness, she's really good. She's completely and totally better than I expected.

And now . . . my dilemma.

It doesn't make any difference to me how awesome she is. I cannot and will not share the Hi-Steppers with my kleptomaniac stepsister. This is so not how I envisioned my junior year.

Finally, Candy's music stops and she takes a bow. And, wait . . . what is this? Oh, you have got to be kidding me. Valerie is giving Candy a standing ovation. This, of course, causes all of Valerie's protégées to also stand.

Will I look like a straight hater if I don't stand up and clap too?

Umm, yeah. I know. So, now, I'm standing, clapping, and smirking.

After the tryouts, which were completely lame outside of Candy's performance, Mrs. Vaughn wants to meet with Valerie and me to deliberate on who we should select. But until she calls us into her office, we have time to mingle with the other Hi-Steppers. The hopefuls are hanging around too, talking to other members of the squad, trying to get a feel about whether they're going to be picked.

Jewel's cousin Sarah asks, "So, Gia, what did you think of my performance?"

Why did she have to ask me? Sarah's routine was to Britney Spears's song, "Gimme More." She just about nailed Britney's performance on the MTV Video Music Awards. Mmm-hmm. It was that bad. I did *not* want more. No ma'am, I did not.

"What did *you* think of your performance?" I ask, trying to avoid giving an answer that might hurt her feelings.

A big smile burst onto Sarah's face. "I thought it totally rocked!"

I am now completely in blank stare mode. What am I supposed to say to that? That's what I get for asking the question.

"Well, rock on then!" I know that was a lame, cop-out response, but it's all I could come up with.

Sarah looks pleased, though. I hope I didn't give her the wrong impression, because she is.soooo not getting picked for the A or B squad. If we had a Z squad, then maybe . . .

Mrs. Vaughn has finally poked her head out of her office door. "Valerie, Gia! Come on back. The rest of you ladies are dismissed. We'll have the results posted in two days."

Valerie and I jog back to Mrs. Vaughn's office and take seats in front of her desk. Mrs. Vaughn has her selection sheet already marked up and there are big red lines through several of the names. Sarah's name is already crossed through, which means Valerie and I won't have to deliberate on her. Thank the Lord up in the heavens!

Candy's name has a green circle around it. That means she's made Mrs. Vaughn's short list. Dang.

Mrs. Vaughn says, "I think we had a few stand-out performances this year. That Candy Ferguson was spectacular. And she's a freshman too!"

"Yes, she was *really* good," Valerie adds.

I say, "She was all right."

Both Valerie and Mrs. Vaughn look at me like I've completely lost my mind.

Valerie asks, "Are you serious, Gia? You sound like a hater."

I clear my throat and reply, "Her dad just married my mom, so I don't want to give her any special treatment."

Valerie's eyes light up and she has an expression on her face that I can't quite read.

Mrs. Vaughn says, "Well, I like her. She's a definite on the A squad. It sounds like Valerie agrees."

This here is a touchy scenario for me as the newly crowned co-captain. I wonder if I have any real power. Should I threaten to drop off the squad if they pick Candy? I don't know. What if they tell me to bounce? That would be all bad.

Dang!

"Well, I don't mind if you all don't mind," I reply, trying not to sound as disappointed as I feel.

"It's settled then," Mrs. Vaughn says. "Candy is a lock for the A squad, and we've got one more slot to fill there. My suggestion is the sophomore, Dionna Williams."

Valerie scrunches her nose. "She can step, but her reputation is kind of tarnished. The Hi-Steppers are supposed to be examples for the young ladies in the school."

Mrs. Vaughn raises her eyebrows and I know my eyes are about to pop out of my head. Valerie is full of jokes today. She is just about the last person to talk about someone's reputation.

"None of the stories about me have ever been confirmed," Valerie says as if she's reading my mind.

Mrs. Vaughn shakes her head. "At any rate, Valerie, I don't think I'm going to hold rumors over this young lady's head. We'll post the list day after tomorrow, but I expect the both of you to keep our selections confidential."

"Of course, Mrs. Vaughn," Valerie says.

I nod my head in agreement as well. I have absolutely no plans to tell Candy anything. Hopefully something will take place between now and Wednesday that will make this nightmare disappear.

★ 8 ★

Tonight is youth choir rehearsal night, and although it's a school night I'm up in the spot along with Hope, Ricky, Kevin and, unfortunately, Candy. She is determined to become my evil doppelganger (yeah, that's an SAT word fo' sho') and do everything that I do. Hi-Steppers, check! Youth choir, check! Next thing you know she'll be . . .

Oh, wait half a darn minute. This heifer has just taken her jacket off and she has the audacity to be rocking a Tweety T-shirt. And it's not just any Tweety. It's my *favorite* powder blue, glitter Tweety with the words *Fabulous Me* on the front.

Yeah, I hear what you're saying. And yes, I do have a new look for this school year. But Tweety has not been retired. Our bond is too strong for that! He is simply on hiatus.

Just as I'm about to step to Candy and check her, Hope slides up in my area. "Hey, Gia," she says.

"Hello."

Hope asks, "Why are you looking extra heated?"

I am so furious that I cannot even form the words. I just glare over in Candy's direction and Hope follows my eyes.

"What?" Hope asks. She apparently doesn't see anything out of place.

I say one word. "Tweety."

Hope's lips form a little O and her eyes widen. "She's wearing your shirt! Did she ask you?"

I lift an eyebrow and give Hope a grimace. Like I'd be angry if she'd asked. Of course, if she'd asked, I would've said no. But I still wouldn't be angry.

"So I guess this isn't a good time to tell you my news," Hope says, sounding disappointed.

I suppose I can deal with the criminal later. "What's your news?"

Hope smiles widely. "You are officially looking at a Longfellow Spartans rally girl!"

"Do they even have tryouts?" I ask. This is a valid question, by the way. How much talent does it take to pass out party flyers and chase boys?

"Yes, they have tryouts! You have to prove that you have spirit. And I've got spirit!"

At that very moment Kevin walks up. "Did you say you have the Holy Spirit?"

Both Hope and I give Kevin blank stares. Of course she didn't say that, but do you know anyone who would stand in the church and say anything about *not* having the Holy Spirit?

Something is different about Kevin. I twist my lips to one side, trying to concentrate. Nope, it's not his clothes.

Corduroy pants and a tucked-in monster truck T-shirt—
still a hot mess. It's not his hands, because I can tell they're
moist and glistening from where I'm standing.

Ah! I see what it is! Kevin's glasses are missing. I wonder if Mother Cranford prayed one of her healing prayers
over him, because he is almost completely blind without
those thick bifocals.

"Kevin, where are your glasses?" I ask.

"I have contacts now!" he exclaims. "What do you
think? Do you like them?"

Well . . . I don't dislike them, that's for sure. It's like
I'm seeing Kevin's face for the first time ever, and it's not
all that bad. He's not fine or anything, but he's got that
nerd cute, Lupe Fiasco kinda look. Trust, Kevin's got a
long way to go in the swagger department, but losing the
glasses is mos def a step in the right direction.

"You look nice, Kevin," I decide to reply. After all of
the insults I've hurled at him, there is no reason why I
can't throw him a compliment every now and then.

It's the Christian thing to do.

Kevin's face turns beet red. "Thank you, Gia!"

He then runs toward the pulpit where we practice,
probably to share the good news about my change of
heart with Ricky.

Hope giggles. "Gia, Kevin just might turn out to be
halfway decent."

"Perhaps," I shrug.

"You think maybe one day you and Kev will double
date with me and Ricky?"

I give her a tremendous amount of my why-you-sound-
stupid side eye and march myself on up to the pulpit.

That foolishness was not funny and I don't like to speak things that are not, as though they are—not in the house of the Lord. This is the place where impossible miracles occur.

I choose to stop thinking about this half-improved Kevin and focus my attention on Brother Bryan. He is only twenty-five, so if he really wanted to, he could wait for me to graduate from high school and marry me. Wow . . . that totally sounds like something that would morph Gwen into her ninja stance.

Brother Bryan says, "I want everyone to welcome the newest member of our youth choir. Sister Candy Ferguson! Y'all give her a hand."

Everyone claps but me. I can't bring myself to do it. I don't welcome her to yet another one of my activities. Why doesn't she just find something that she likes on her own? Can't she have just one original thought?

We rehearse for exactly one hour. Brother Bryan is strict about this during the school year. He doesn't want any of us to blame him for slipping grades.

My uncle, Pastor Robert, drives Candy and me home. Usually Hope rides with us, but since Aunt Elena was finishing work at the church tonight, she goes home with her mom.

Once we're driving down the street, Pastor asks, "So how are you and Gwen settling in to your new home?"

I glance over my shoulder into the backseat. "I don't really feel like it's my home. It seems like I'm just visiting."

I think of the picture of the poor man on the Monopoly board who's stuck in jail, and the words *Just Visiting* on the outside. Only thing is, my situation is the opposite. I'm the one stuck behind the bars, and I don't have any idea how long it's going to take for me to get released.

"What about me, Pastor Stokes? Don't you want to hear about how I'm adjusting?" Candy asks.

"Of course I do!" Pastor Stokes exclaims. "What do you think of the new additions to your family?"

"Well, Gwen is kinda nice. She pretty much leaves me alone."

Pastor smiles. "And what about Gia?"

Yes. What about me? I dare her to say something out of pocket.

"I don't think Gia likes me at all. She didn't want to share a room with me, and just a little while ago, she threatened to beat me down if I wore any more of her cartoon character T-shirts."

I gasp. "If you're gonna snitch, do it correctly. I said I was going to bring the pain if I saw you wearing my T-shirts again. And we're not just talking about any cartoon character, we're talking about Tweety. Pastor, you know how I feel about Tweety."

"I see. Well, I don't want either of you resorting to violence. God would not be pleased with that at all. But Candy, do you think you could ask Gia first before borrowing her things?"

Candy slams against the backseat and pouts. "She wouldn't have let me if I'd asked."

"You're right! I wouldn't have. I don't share Tweety!" I yell.

"See how mean she is?"

"Do either of you know what it means to be long-suffering?"

Oh no! Our bickering has triggered a Pastor Stokes mini-sermon. Candy is not familiar with how this works, but I totally am. If I had a nickel for every one of these sermons that Hope and I have gotten over the years, I could afford those designer outfits that Candy likes to get for free.

"It's one of the fruits of the Spirit. You should know what it means, Gia—we've discussed it in Bible study," Pastor Stokes says.

I laugh. "That's easy. It means to put up with some-one's mess for a long time. Like my entire life."

"There's more to it than that, Gia. It's not just putting up with the mess. It's putting up with it patiently. Are you being patient with your sister?"

"No," I reply, my face twisted into a grimace.

"What about you, Candy? Gia is used to being an only child. Are you patiently waiting for Gia to come around and be more generous with her things?"

Candy responds, "No, I guess not."

"The only way the both of you are going to get along, is if you decide to be long-suffering toward one another."

Talk about long-suffering . . . I'm patiently awaiting the end of this speech.

Pastor Stokes laughs as he pulls into our driveway. "Okay, Gia. I see you rolling your eyes, now. I'm done."

"Thank you!"

Candy and I get out of the car and start up the walk.

She smirks at me and rolls her eyes. I give it right back to her.

"So are you going to tell me?" Candy asks.

"Tell you what?"

"Did I make the Hi-Steppers squad?"

I throw back my head and laugh. This girl is hilarious. She borrows my shirt without asking, then snitches on me to my uncle, and on top of all that she wants me to give her insider information? Is she serious?

"You'll find out tomorrow with everyone else."

Candy frowns and stomps away from me. As she steps onto the porch she spins around with both hands on her hips and screams, "I really, really can't stand you, Gia."

I reply, "Ditto, Candy. Di-tto!"

★ 9 ★

This year, I have the great, great pleasure of having English class with Ricky and . . . wait for it . . . my knight in shining moisture . . . Kevin. He sits behind me, and Ricky is in the next row.

We're waiting for our teacher, Ms. Beckman, to start the class. It looks like she's out in the hall flirting with one of the security guards. I am not mad at her! Go ahead with your *fresh* self, Ms. Beckman.

"Choir rehearsal was fun last night, wasn't it, Gia?" Kevin asks.

See, this is why he gets on my nerves. It's not that choir rehearsal wasn't fun, but Kevin just wants everyone to know that we hang out after school hours and over the weekend. I don't even know why he does it! It's not like anyone cares what I do when I'm not at school.

"It was choir rehearsal, Kev. How much fun could it be?"

He replies, "Well, I don't know about you, but I enjoy lifting up the name of my Lord and Savior."

Ricky's eyes light up. "Speaking of fun, are we going to Cedar Point on Saturday? Everyone in the junior class is supposed to be there."

It's a Longfellow High tradition for the upperclassmen to go to Cedar Point on Labor Day weekend. It's pretty much the last weekend of the summer and Cedar Point is the only real amusement park anywhere near Cleveland, and it's about an hour and a half away. I didn't even think about trying to go last year, but it sounds like fun.

"I'm down," I say enthusiastically. "Are you driving, Ricky?"

"Of course! You rolling with us, Kev?"

Kevin grins. "Only if Gia wants me to go."

"What if I say I want you to stay at home?" I ask.

A frown contorts Kevin's face. "Why would you say that, Gia? You're supposed to be my friend."

"Yep, and I'm going to put you on friendship time-out if you keep up your foolishness."

"Okay," Kevin pouts. "I'm sorry."

I reply, "You're forgiven, and of course I want you to go. It wouldn't be any fun without you, Kevin!"

Kevin smiles so hard that his eyes narrow to little slits. "Good! 'Cause I'm coming! I'm gonna win you a bear, Gia," he says, still smiling.

"Hope can ride with us too, but we've gotta split the gas. Is that cool?" Ricky asks.

"That's cool with me. Mother Cranford is gonna trip about me not being there on Saturday, and I can't go Friday night because we've got a game."

Ricky says, "Maybe you should try to go today. I'll help you, if you want."

"Nah, that's okay," I say. "You have football practice."

Everyone in our circle and at our church are super thrilled about Ricky being the starting quarterback this season. He's shown so much promise, along with a running back, James, that there were scouts from Division I schools in our stands at the very first game.

"Don't you have Hi-Steppers practice?" Kevin asks.

"Yep, but Mrs. Vaughn will let me go early if I tell her it's for Mother Cranford."

Kevin looks at his watch, "Where is Ms. Beckman? I am here to learn, not to watch her make a love connection!"

"Chill out, Kevin," I say with a giggle. I wonder if he made that funny on purpose or if it was accidental.

"Anyway, I was thinking we should get hotel rooms up in Sandusky instead of trying to ride back from the park late at night," Ricky says.

"Do you really think Gwen is gonna let me stay in a hotel room overnight without a chaperone? Plus, don't you have to be at least eighteen to get a hotel room?"

Ricky shrugs. "Brother Bryan is going and taking some of the young people from the church. He said he'd get the rooms for us. Why don't you just ask Gwen? It's not like you'll be in the same room with boys. My parents already said yes."

"I'll ask, but I'm definitely not making any promises."

"Okay."

Jewel and Kelani poke their heads inside our classroom and shout out, "Ooo-OOO!"

"Ooo-OOO!" I shout.

Ricky laughs. "Y'all sound like a flock of carrier pigeons."

"Do not hate, Ricky."

"That's cool how you got Candy on the squad. I saw her in the hallway celebrating with her crew."

I reply angrily, "I did not get her on the squad. If it was up to me she wouldn't even be riding the bench. I don't need her participating in my extracurricular activities."

"Aw, Gia, don't be like that. She just wants to be like you. What's so wrong with that?"

"I'm unique, Ricky. Nobody needs a second Gia up in the spot. One Gia is absolutely sufficient."

Ricky cocks his head to the side and smiles. "Okay. Maybe you're right."

Ms. Beckman finally closes the door to our classroom. I guess she got a date or something because she is grinning from ear to ear.

Someone from the back of the class yells, "Did you get them digits, Ms. B?"

She tosses her long, straight, Barbie-doll-blond hair over her shoulder and replies, "That is for me to know and you *not* to know."

Ms. Beckman continues, "Are you all ready for your first assignment of the school year?"

A collective groan rises up from our class. I guess I'm the only one who likes writing essays. Even Kevin is shaking his head in disgust.

"I just *love* your enthusiasm!" Ms. Beckman exclaims. "It is so refreshing."

She goes around to the other side of her desk and pulls out a stack of romance novels. She holds them up for everyone to see.

"What do you all think these are?"

Kevin says, "Those are the books they sell at the super-market."

"Yes," Ms. Beckman replies, "these are romance novels. I bet you all are wondering what these books have to do with eleventh-grade English."

She needs to hurry up and explain where she's going with this. There was not one romance novel on our advanced placement reading list. And if she says we're reading this stuff, trust and believe Gwen will be up here with a quickness.

Ms. Beckman says, "Romance novels have a formula. Boy meets girl, something happens to keep boy from girl, boy and girl work out their differences, and finally boy and girl live happily ever after."

Okay, what part of the game is this? I still can't tell what this has to do with a sista's SAT scores. She betta quit playing.

"For our first writing assignment of the year, I want us to do something fun!" Ms. Beckman continues. "We're going to write our own romantic short stories."

"Do our stories have to follow that formula?" someone asks.

"No, not at all. You can follow the tried and true romance formula or you can invent your own. The only rule is that these stories should be works of fiction. Anyone who uses their friends as an inspiration will receive an F."

Ricky has a doubtful expression on his face. "Can we work in groups?" he asks.

"Absolutely," Ms. Beckman replies. "You may work in pairs or groups of three. The stories should be at least two thousand words and the most entertaining story will appear in the fall edition of the student newspaper. So, go ahead and form your groups. Happy writing!"

Kevin leans forward. "Gia, will you work with me?"

"Sure. Ricky, you want to make this thing a trio?"

Ricky smiles. "Only if Kevin wants me to be in your group."

I'm going to do bodily harm to Ricky, right here and right now. It is totally his fault that Kevin has not gotten over his crush on me. Ricky says little stuff like this that continues to give Kevin hope, when, alas, there is none.

"Of course Kevin doesn't mind. Isn't that right, Kev?"

Kevin says, "That's cool, Ricky."

Why does Kevin sound disappointed? Boo!

After English class is dismissed, it's off to Hi-Steppers rehearsal. We are doing our first new routine on Friday and it was, of course, choreographed by me. This is also the first rehearsal that includes the newbies—Candy and Dionna.

I usually am the first one to rehearsal, but eager beaver Candy has beat me here and is talking up a storm to Mrs. Vaughn. Instead of her signature thick braid, Candy has her hair in two pigtails with ribbons on the ends. I quickly scan her outfit as well. She better be glad she's not wearing anything that belongs to me.

Valerie sashays into the girl's locker room and immediately I see the inspiration for Candy's hairstyle. Valerie has her long brown hair parted down the middle and in two braids that she's pulled over her shoulders. Not surprisingly, there are two small ribbons at the end of each braid.

"Ooo-OOO!" Valerie calls.

"Ooo-OOO," I reply. "You ready for Friday?"

"Of course I am. What about you?"

"You know it!"

Valerie carefully hangs her designer blouse in her locker and pulls a Spartans T-shirt over her head. "What's up with my boyfriend?" she asks.

"Who, Brad? I heard he went off to college."

Valerie plops down next to me on the bench. "Not Brad. I'm talking about Ricky. I heard a rumor that your cousin is checking for him. Is that true?"

I swallow hard. So now Hope is shouting her crush from the rooftops. Wow. Well, as long as she doesn't keep asking me to be a part of her drama, I'm cool.

"She did mention something about thinking that Ricky was cute. That's about it."

"That's it?" Valerie asks in a high-pitched voice. "Didn't you think you should mention that to me?"

I suck in my top lip and shake my head. "Why would I tell you about that?"

"Because of the rule. Hi-Steppers don't share boys . . . ever."

"Hope is not a Hi-Stepper."

"But she was, and once you're a Hi-Stepper, you're always a Hi-Stepper," Valerie replies.

A little chuckle escapes my lips. "Okay, let me get this straight. Hope gets completely humiliated by you and the rest of the Hi-Steppers, so much that she quits the squad. And now you expect her to still follow your rules?"

Valerie nods. "Yes, absolutely. And if you help her hook up with Ricky, you're also in violation of the rules."

I stand and start walking toward the gym. "Valerie, you really need to think about that foolishness you just invented. I won't have anything to do with Hope and Ricky hooking up, but it has nothing to do with your rules."

"What is it then?" asks Valerie. "Do you want him for yourself?"

"No, Valerie. Everyone is not your competition."

Valerie seems satisfied with my somewhat truthful response. I don't want Ricky for myself, not now anyway. But not because I think he won't make a great boyfriend. It's mostly because I think it would be an exercise in futility (you know how I feel about giving definitions . . . expand your vocab!).

In the gym, Candy is helping Dionna get a complex part of our Friday-night routine down. I have to admit that Candy is truly an asset to the squad. She and I have been practicing at home together, too. It's the only time we're not arguing.

"Y'all almost have it, but let me show you that clap/kick combination one more time," I say.

I stand in front of them and demonstrate the intricate move, and wait for them to copy me. Jewel and Kelani join us as well, because neither of them have it down either.

Wait a minute, something is not right with this picture. Oh, now I see. Jewel and Kelani, as usual, are sporting matching hairstyles. Today they have afro puffs. Yes, you

heard it correctly. Jewel has two giant bulks of blond syn-
thetic braided hair attached to her very straight European
hair. The result is a mess. An utter train wreck of a hot-
foot mess.

"Why y'all trying to swagger jack me?" I ask Kelani.

"What?"

"The afro puffs?"

Kelani pats her own puffs, which are several shades
lighter than her own hair. "You like?" she asks.

"Umm, no!" says Valerie, finally joining us from the
locker room. "We're only having one puff princess on this
squad and that's going to be Gia. If you two wear your
hair like that on Friday, you're gonna be on the bench."

"Don't hate, Valerie. Participate!" Jewel says.

We practice the routine over and over again, until it is
perfect. Even Mrs. Vaughn is impressed with how it comes
together. We're going to look extra hot on Friday night.

Everyone goes to the locker room to get dressed. I'm
trying to ignore the chatter, because I have to rush myself
over to Mother Cranford's as soon as I leave here.

Valerie holds up a very colorfully decorated piece of
paper. "It looks like the rally girls are having a post-game
party Friday night."

"But we always go to IHOP after the games," Jewel
says.

Valerie nods. "Yes, we do. It sounds like the rally girls
are trying to compete with our tradition."

"Wait, don't the rally girls always have post-game parties?" I ask.

Kelani replies, "Yes, during basketball season. Football
season belongs to the Hi-Steppers."

"Why would they want to challenge us?" asks Candy.

Valerie balls the flyer up and throws it into the trash can. "There's only one person who would want to wreck our flow."

"Who?" asks Jewel.

"Think about it," Valerie says. "Who wanted so badly to be a Hi-Stepper that she had us looking foolish on the field? Who quit the squad because she didn't want to sit on the bench? Who joined the rally girls this year, because the Hi-Steppers didn't want her back?"

I roll my eyes and sigh. Clearly, Valerie is speaking about Hope. If Hope is behind any of this, I've got a suspicion that it has nothing to do with getting revenge on the Hi-Steppers, but everything to do with a certain football player crush.

Kelani squeals, "Ooh, Candy! Those jeans are cute."

"Yes, they are," Valerie comments. "You're wearing Lucky jeans? Wow, Gia, your new stepdaddy must be ballin' for real."

I glare angrily at Candy. There is no way Elder LeRon bought her those two-hundred-dollar jeans. She looks back at me, her eyes pleading for me not to tell her secret.

I clear my throat. "If he's ballin', I sure can't tell. He must be giving all of the shopping money to his precious little baby."

"Umm . . . my mom bought them for me," Candy says with a nervous giggle.

"Well, Gia, you need to pick up some fashion tips from your little sister," Valerie says. "She's looking flawless right now, from head to toe."

Candy smiles adoringly at Valerie. "Thank you, Val! I'm glad you like my outfit."

"Don't get too thankful, boo. It's not a good look. We are Hi-Steppers and we're supposed to be fierce," Valerie says.

I stand up and grab my gym bag. "I've got to go. Mother Cranford is waiting. And Candy, you need to get to the house. It's spaghetti night."

Candy scrunches her nose. "Is that *all* your mother cooks?"

"Just be glad it isn't tuna surprise night."

★ 10 ★

Gwen is sitting at the kitchen table doing a crossword puzzle in the newspaper. This is great, because it means she's in chill mode. I need her to be completely relaxed because I'm about to ask her about going to Cedar Point.

"Mom, I need to ask you something," I say.

Gwen places her pencil on the table and pats one of the chairs. "Come on in here and sit down," she says.

I sit at the table and take a sip out of Gwen's glass. She snatches her glass of juice away from me and sips it herself. For a second, it feels like old times when it was just me and Gwen. No husband, no pilfering stepsister. Just the two of us.

"What do you want to ask me?"

"Will you please listen to the entire request before you say anything?" I ask.

Gwen shakes her head. "Unh-uh! Nope. Whenever you say something like that, you're about to ask me something ridiculous."

"Mom! Just hear me out."

"Go ahead, Gia. But this better not be crazy."

"Well, most of the junior class is going to Cedar Point over Labor Day weekend."

Gwen twists her lips to the side and squints. "And? What else?" she asks.

"I'd like to go. Ricky said he would drive if we gave him gas money."

"Okay, you can go," Gwen says.

"Thanks, Mom, but that's not all."

"There's more?"

"Well, yes. If we stay until the park closes, it will be too late for us to drive an hour and a half coming back home."

Gwen crosses her arms like she knows what's coming. I continue. "So Brother Bryan, the youth choir director, has agreed to chaperone us if we get a few hotel rooms and stay the night. We'd be back for Sunday morning worship service."

"Is that this coming weekend?" asks Gwen.

"No, it's next weekend."

"Well, you-all sure have this all planned out, don't you?"

"Please, Mom! Please, can I go?" I beg.

"Can you go where?" Elder LeRon asks. He's walked into the house and right up into a conversation where he was not invited.

"Hi, honey!" says Gwen. "Some of the young people

from the church are going to Cedar Point on Labor Day weekend."

Elder LeRon frowns. "What young people?"

"Brother Bryan is taking a few car groups," I reply. I do not appreciate this interrogation. Not one bit.

"Is Candy going?" he asks.

"Umm, no!"

Gwen asks, "Why can't Candy go?"

"Yes, why isn't your stepsister invited?"

I can't stop the groan that escapes my mouth. First of all, why is LeRon even a part of this conversation? I'm not asking him for his permission, I'm asking my mother for *her* permission.

"She's not invited because she's a freshman, and no freshmen are invited. This is an upperclassmen event," I explain.

"That's silly," Gwen says. "Candy's only a little bit younger than you. It'll be just as much fun with her there."

Candy pokes her head out of our bedroom. "What are you all talking about? I heard my name," she says.

"Did you hear about this trip to Cedar Point?" asks Elder LeRon.

Candy replies, "Yes, I heard about it, and I don't really want to go. It's gonna be a bunch of juniors. I'd rather go to the mall with my friends."

Elder LeRon frowns. "If Candy isn't going, then Gia isn't going."

"Mom! That's not fair!" I know I'm whining, but I can't help it.

"LeRon, I don't think Gia should miss out on the fun just because Candy isn't interested in going."

"Are there going to be boys there?" asks Elder LeRon.

"Yes, there are. Ricky is going to drive," answers Gwen.

"Do you honestly think we can trust Gia not to do something irresponsible?" Elder LeRon asks.

Gwen narrows her eyes angrily. "I trust Gia, LeRon."

"Well, I don't, not after last year."

"I believe that everyone deserves a second chance," Gwen says.

"Okay, Gia. You're allowed to go to Cedar Point. But if you do anything to betray our trust, you won't see the outside of this house until you graduate from high school."

Gwen gets up from the table and goes into the kitchen to heat up the spaghetti that she's cooked for dinner. LeRon and I stay in the living room, staring each other up and down.

It's so ironic that he thinks I'm some kind of promiscuous teen delinquent, and his daughter is the one with the sticky fingers. I'm sick of the staring contest so I get up from the table as well.

"Mom, I've got some homework. Can you call me when dinner is ready?"

I go into the bedroom that I share with Candy and slam the door. She's standing next to her desk, folding a stack of clothes that still have the tags on them.

"Been shopping?" I ask sarcastically.

Candy doesn't reply. She just smiles and puts her new clothes away.

"You might want to check that, Candy. I hear that kind of thing is addictive."

Candy rolls her eyes. "Don't start in on me, Gia. You've got beef with my father, not me."

"Well, maybe if he knew what you were doing, he wouldn't have time to harass me."

"Are you going to snitch on me?" Candy asks.

"I'm considering it."

"Stop tripping, Gia. Why don't you just make a shopping list and let me boost you a few things. It wouldn't be any trouble at all."

Laughter bubbles up from my throat. "Girl, you aren't taking me down with you! No, ma'am!"

"I was only offering to be nice, Gia. My dad will never believe you if you tell him about this."

I wave my hand over her stolen goods. "The evidence is right here. I don't have to convince him."

"Do you actually think I haven't thought about getting caught? I'll just say that they belong to a friend or that my mom's new boyfriend bought them."

That would be totally believable too, because Candy's mom feels guilty for shipping her off to LeRon's, so she buys gifts to make up for it. It kind of sucks for Candy.

I shake my head in disgust and plop down on my bed. Everything Candy said is true. Even if I did snitch on her, especially right now, it would just look like I'm trying to divert attention away from me.

There's a light knock on the door. That's nobody but Gwen. Candy stuffs all the rest of her booty (not like badonkadunk, but like pirate's *booty*) into the dresser drawer.

"Come in," I say.

Gwen steps inside and closes the door lightly. She looks annoyed, as if she and LeRon continued their conversation about me after I left the room. I'm actually proud of my mother because she's doing her best to be a good wife and to take care of me at the same time.

"So, LeRon and I decided that we should go to Cedar Point as a family. You can hang with your friends, but we'll be there to chaperone."

I let out a groan. Being a junior in high school and having your mama chaperone you is definitely not the business.

Gwen continues, "Miss Candy, you can forget about seeing your friends on Labor Day weekend. We're all going to go to Cedar Point."

"Is there any way I can keep this disaster from happening?" I ask.

"Gia, it won't be that bad. Cedar Point is huge. You don't have to see us for the entire day if you don't want to."

Why does she not understand the principle of the matter? This is all about LeRon trying to control me, and him proving to my mother that I can't be trusted.

Candy says, "It'll be cool, Gia. We can wear matching outfits."

Take me, Lord. Take me now.

Ricky, Kevin, and I are sitting at our favorite table in the cafeteria, and we're discussing our project for English class. Kevin has a fresh haircut *and* a new outfit that is just a little bit fly. He's seriously trying to step up his game, and I ain't mad at him.

"So, what if we write the story about a damsel in distress who's rescued by a handsome guy and then they fall in love?" offers Ricky.

"Umm . . . boring!" I reply. "How about we have a girl rescue a boy from his lame existence. Then he tries to get with her and she says . . . no thanks!"

Kevin scrunches his nose. "That doesn't sound like a romance. That sounds like a story about a mean girl."

I toss my hand into the air. "Okay, whatever! We can write a typical story if y'all want. I don't care. I've got bigger fish to fry."

"Like what?" asks Ricky.

"Like Gwen and her little man LeRon crashing our Cedar Point trip."

Ricky gasps. "What?"

"Yeah. Feel my pain, bro. They are definitely tripping."

Kevin shrugs. "It's not that bad, Gia. It's not like we were going to do anything bad."

"Yeah, but having them there is embarrassing."

Kevin replies, "Well, it could be worse. It could be my grandparents."

Ooh. Yeah, Kevin is right. I can see Mother Witherspoon now, handing us fried chicken sandwiches out of her purse with big hunks of pound cake in sandwich bags. That would be all sorts of bad.

"So, are you going to the rally girls' party after the game?" Ricky asks.

My eyes widen with surprise. "No! Are you going? What about IHOP?"

"Well, I don't have to go to IHOP. Plus, Hope invited me, so I'm thinking I'll go."

Kevin asks, "Am I invited too?"

"If I am, then you are!" says Ricky. "That's how we roll."

"Wait a minute! What about the Hi-Steppers? We always chill at IHOP after the game."

Ricky laughs. "Gia, since when did you care what the rest of the Hi-Steppers are doing? Why don't you hang with us at the rally girls' bowling party?"

Aw, dang. I love bowling. I actually love bowling more than I love any of the Hi-Steppers or those extra fluffy pancakes at IHOP.

"Cosmic bowling?" I ask.

"Yep," Ricky replies. "It's gonna be dark and the fluo-rescent lights are gonna be on! It should be fresh, for real."

Something just occurred to me—a reason why Ricky might be upsetting the delicate balance of high school politics. He thinks he's slick, but he is sooo the opposite.

"Ricky, are you trying to avoid Valerie?" I ask.

He nearly chokes on a French fry. "Umm, no. Why would I be avoiding her?"

"Because you really liked her last year, and she played you like a dummy," Kevin says.

Ricky protests, "She did not play me like a dummy. I knew what she was doing all along."

Kevin and I both give Ricky a huge dose of dude-quit-playing side eye. If I recall correctly, Ricky's nose was so open you could drive a Hummer through it.

"All right, I dug her a little bit, but it wasn't all like how ya'll are talking," Ricky says.

We still refuse to agree and let Ricky off the hook.

"Okay," Ricky says. "I really liked her, and you're right, Gia. I don't want to go to IHOP if she's going to be there."

"What if I told you that Valerie is really sorry for what she did, and that she might want to get back with you?"

Ricky looks like he's just seen a ghost. "Are you seri-ous?"

"Would I lie about something like this?" I ask.

Ricky takes another French fry and pops it into his mouth. He chews slowly as if he's thinking. Honestly, I didn't expect too much pondering to take place on this Valerie scenario. She played him bad, so I didn't think she had a chance at all.

"I don't think she means it," Ricky says. "Valerie only thinks about herself."

I cannot and will not disagree with that statement. It's Valerie's fault for digging this hole. But at least I've kept my word. I mentioned it to Ricky; now she can do the rest.

Since today is a game day, we have an afternoon pep rally. Everyone gets dressed in uniform and we all go into the auditorium for a lot of screaming, yelling, and cheering. Actually, it's pretty fun.

I march into the gym with all of the other Hi-Steppers, including Candy. We're doing a simple step around the floor to the beat of the music provided by the marching band.

The cheerleaders run into the gym after us. They are totally upstaging the Hi-Steppers with all of those cartwheels and whatnot. We need to step it up a notch, for real.

Okay, I'm almost one hundred percent sure I didn't say that out loud. But Candy must've been reading my mind, because this heifer just did about four backflips down the center of the floor. Everyone's cheering, especially the freshmen section.

The rally girls are next into the gymnasium. Since when do they have uniforms? They're wearing tiny red shorts and white baby tees that say *Spartans* across their chests. The cutest thing about their outfits are their little gladiator hats. They've also got tiny red pom-poms that they're waving all over the place.

Hope runs to the middle of the floor and starts a chant. "We're here to pep you up! We're here to pep you up! Because the Spartans are gonna wreck it up!"

All right now! My cousin has spirit, y'all. She's more pumped out there with the rally girls than she ever was as a Hi-Stepper. I think she's found her calling.

"What is *she* doing?" Valerie asks.

I cover my mouth to keep from giggling. Valerie is extra heated. She doesn't like anyone trying to steal her shine, and Hope is pretty much doing just that.

So Valerie starts the Hi-Steppers call, "Ooo-OOO!"

"Ooo-OOO!" the Hi-Steppers reply.

Valerie steps to the center of the floor and cups her hands around her mouth. She yells out to the crowd, "I said Ooo-OOO!"

A loud *Ooo-OOO* comes from the bleachers. Valerie signals to the rest of the Hi-Steppers to follow her to the middle of the floor. She leads us in a fresh, spur-of-the-moment step that blows the rally girls out of the water. They take their tiny pom-poms and go off to the side where they belong.

Valerie whispers to me as the football team enters, "This is *our* house! Hi-Steppers, chica!"

When Ricky runs into the gym, everyone stands. He smiles and waves. Hope starts up another chant with the rally girls.

"Ri-cky! Ri-cky!" they chant.

Ricky grins at the rally girls and waves at them. I glance at Valerie out of the corner of my eye, to see what her reaction is going to be. She narrows her eyes slowly and inhales deeply.

"Does your cousin like Ricky?" Valerie whispers.

"Who doesn't like Ricky? He's a really cool dude."

"Don't try to play me, Gia. Are they talking? Is your cousin with Ricky?" Valerie asks. I can hear the nervousness in her tone. This is so unlike Valerie.

I answer truthfully. "They are not together, Valerie. Maybe Hope likes him, but he hasn't paid her any attention at all."

Valerie smiles wickedly. "Well, if she thinks her little rally girl squad is going to help her take my boo, she can forget about it."

Her boo! Ricky? Wow on top of wow.

"I don't think Ricky is even feeling you, Valerie, to be honest," I say.

Valerie's smile spreads. "That is only temporary, trust me."

At that very moment Valerie catches Ricky's attention, stands on her tiptoes and waves at him. And then he shocks the dummy out of me by waving back.

Wow to infinity.

After the pep rally, there's a mad rush to the locker room, so that we can change out of our uniforms before they get ruined for game night. Plus the cheerleaders will hog all of the space if we don't stake our claim first.

Most of the Hi-Steppers make it into the locker room in time to chat before our last-period class. Mine is Government, so trust and believe I'm in absolutely no hurry.

Kelani asks, "So, Val, are you driving us to Cedar Point?"

"I guess. I was hoping to ride along with my new boo, but that's definitely not happening," Valerie replies while giving me the you-didn't-hook-me-up side eye. Whatever!

Candy says, "Oh, I think I'm riding with my dad. He and my stepmother are coming along."

"Eww! Your *parents* are coming?" Jewel asks.

"Yeah. I guess they don't trust Gia to spend the night all the way in Sandusky," Candy says.

Valerie gives me a strange look. "Gia, you're spending the night? Who else is in this little posse?"

"Some people from my church," I reply vaguely.

"Ricky goes to your church," Kelani says, stating the obvious.

I nod. "And a gold star goes to Kelani. Does anyone else want to try for the silver?"

Valerie crosses her eyes and squints angrily. "Spill it, Gia. You're spending the night in Sandusky with Ricky and who else?"

"Oh, for crying out loud! It's gonna be me, Ricky, Hope, Kevin, Candy, and some other people that y'all don't know from our church."

"My man is spending the night in Sandusky and you didn't think I'd be interested in knowing that?" Valerie asks.

I'm going to need her to stop calling Ricky "her man." It sounds kind of obsessive and stalker-like. She's reminding me of Nikki Parker chasing down Professor Ogilvie on *The Parkers* TV show.

"Well, you know now, Valerie. Are you coming with?"

Valerie smirks. "Yes, I suppose I will. Kelani and Jewel can ride with me."

I grab up my stuff and make a mad dash for the hall. I am so not trying to be late to class.

I wonder how Ricky is going to handle both of his lady loves in one setting. Hope is thirsty and Valerie is extra thirsty. Maybe it would help if he *knew* they were his lady loves! But then again, it probably wouldn't.

★ 12 ★

"**A**re you all ready?" Valerie asks the Hi-Steppers squad.

"Ooo-OOO!" we all yell in unison.

"Well, then, let's rock this. Some misguided Longfellow Spartans seem to think that they are the spirit ambassadors of this school! But whose job is it to get the team pumped?"

"Hi-Steppers!"

"That's right!" Valerie says. "Hi-Steppers! Now we're going to help our team get a victory. Let's go!"

On our way out to the field, Kelani whispers to me, "What's up with Valerie? She's like super excited tonight! What do you think that's about?"

I don't answer Kelani, but I know exactly what it's about. Valerie is on a mission to get Ricky.

And Valerie proves what I'm thinking as soon as we

step to the field. She starts her infamous booty popping as she passes the football team, and they all cheer. Well, all except Ricky. But he does have a strange expression on his face that I can't read. It almost looks like he's embarrassed about something.

"Hey, Ricky!" I say as I walk past. He smiles and greets me by pounding my fist.

"Hey, Gi-Gi! What it do?"

I can't help but giggle. Ricky sounds ri-darn-diculous every time he tries to be cool. He should just accept and embrace his inner nerd. It would make it so much easier on all of us.

"Boy, quit playing! Have a good game," I reply as I follow the rest of the Hi-Steppers to the band section.

I scan the crowd, looking for Hope and the rally girls. I'm trying to spot them before Valerie does, because she's bound to do something off the hook. After seeing their bowling-party flyers and that little debacle at the pep rally, there's no telling what she might do.

Finally, I see Hope weaving in and out of the stands with an armful of flyers. She's wearing shiny red pants and a little black jacket. It must be part of the new rally girl apparel, because it looks like they're all wearing the same thing. Something tells me that Hope is their new unofficial leader, because she's all about rocking shiny clothing. Me . . . not so much.

Jewel and Kelani sit down next to me, each of them holding a flyer. Kelani asks, "Are you going to this party or are you going to be at IHOP?"

"Where are y'all gonna be?" I ask, not wanting to be the first traitor among the Hi-Steppers.

Jewel scoots really close to me and says, "We asked you first."

"Wait a minute," I say, "are y'all trying to go to the rally girls' party?"

Kelani lowers her voice to a whisper. "It sounds like fun, and *everybody* is going except us! The football players, cheerleaders . . . everybody!"

"So, if we go, who's going to break it to Valerie?" I ask, because this is really the most important question.

Jewel replies, "We think it should be you because you're the co-captain. You can stand up to her without getting bumped down to the B squad."

"I guess I can do it. But you two better have my back! I'm not playing."

Jewel and Kelani give me matching nods. Tonight they have opted for bright gold eye shadow to go along with their ponytails. I wonder if there's such a thing as multiracial twins, because these two had to be separated at birth.

As if on cue, Valerie stomps down the steps holding a handful of crumpled flyers. "Have y'all heard that everybody is going to this party?"

"Everybody but us," Kelani says under her breath.

"What did you say, chica?" Valerie asks.

She's got a stank attitude for real. Her nostrils are flared and her face is a bright shade of red. I guess we can safely say that the rally girls have gone past the point of no return. They are now Valerie's mortal enemies.

I clear my throat and say, "Look, Valerie. We go to IHOP every week. Don't you think for once we could go along with someone else's program?"

"What are you saying, Gia? I do not understand the words that are coming out of your mouth," says Valerie.

"Shall I say it in Spanish, chica?" I ask.

Valerie purses her lips and frowns. "Don't play, Gia. You're going to this lame bowling thing?"

"Yes, and so are Jewel and Kelani . . . right, y'all?"

For once, the nonbiological twins don't seem to be on the same page. Kelani starts a nod, and Jewel is about to shake her head no. Then they each do the opposite gesture, as if they haven't decided.

"Well, which is it? Are you betraying the Hi-Steppers or not?" Valerie demands.

I roll my eyes furiously. "Look, girl. Nobody is betraying the Hi-Steppers. This is about having fun, and it looks like all the fun is going to happen at the rally girls' party. So the three of us are going."

Candy walks up and joins the conversation. "I'll go wherever you go, Valerie. Are we still going to IHOP?"

"Yes, the loyal Hi-Steppers will be at our normal location."

Jewel and Kelani drop their heads sadly. I reply, "Candy, you are going where I go. Do I need to walk over there to my mom and tell her you're trying to sneak off somewhere without me?"

I narrow my eyes and scowl at Candy. If she wants me to keep her klepto behavior a secret then she better not try to side with Valerie. A look of recognition flashes across her face. She *knows* what it is.

Candy says, "Sorry, Val. Gia's right. I do have to go with her, or my dad won't let me go at all."

Valerie's eyes travel to each of our faces. It's not difficult to see that she's furious. She storms away to go and talk to the other seniors on the Hi-Stepper squad. They'll probably go along with whatever Valerie wants.

Jewel says, "Oh my goodness, Gia. You totally rocked just then. Valerie looked mad enough to kick you off the squad."

"She probably will," Candy warned. "And I won't feel sorry for you. Don't you know that Hi-Steppers are supposed to stick together?"

I want to laugh out loud. Candy has clearly become one of Valerie's disciples. I should give her a warning on how fast Valerie can change. Maybe I'll tell her to ask Hope about it.

"She can't kick me off the squad," I say. "I'm a co-captain. But she can kick *you* off the squad, or she can at least recommend it to Mrs. Vaughn. So, I suggest you worry about getting this step right and forget about the after parties."

"Gia!" I hear Kevin calling my name from a few rows behind us. I'm trying my best to pretend that I don't hear him.

"Gia!" he yells again.

Candy laughs. "Hey Gia, your man is calling you."

"Ha, ha," I reply.

"What's up, Kev!" I shout from my seat.

"We're picking teams for bowling tonight! Will you be on mine?"

I roll my eyes. "Sure, Kevin."

"Ew!" Kelani says. "Are there going to be band geeks at the rally girls' party?"

"Band geeks?" I say with a glare. "That's not really cool, Kelani."

Kelani drops her head, shamefaced. "Valerie always clowns the band."

"Well, I don't do everything Valerie does," I reply. "Kevin is my friend, whether he's in the band or not."

Maybe it's time for me to step up and end Valerie's tyranny over the Hi-Steppers. She's got girls like Jewel and Kelani, who are really kinda nice, just being evil for no reason. That's not cool. I'm starting to think Valerie is not a happy person.

After the game, everyone finds a ride over to the bowling alley. Since I'm riding with Ricky, Hope, Kevin, and Candy, Gwen and LeRon let us have an extra hour and a half. We don't have to be home until after midnight, which is sweet!

Ricky is in a great mood, because they won the game, thirty-five to seven. Kevin is in the front seat and Candy is sandwiched between me and Hope.

Hope asks, "So, Ricky, are you looking forward to the Homecoming game? You should really be ready to show your stuff."

"Yep. We're playing Normandy again this year, so I plan on putting a lot of points on the board."

Kevin jumps in. "Speaking of Homecoming, Gia, I need a date, and I think you should go with me."

Clearly, Kevin has lost his mind. Apparently, he has taken Pastor Stokes's *name it and claim it* message way too literally.

"Umm, Kevin. Why'd you have to go and kill the mood, boy?"

Everyone but Kevin bursts into laughter.

"So what about you, Ricky?" Hope asks. "Who are you taking?"

"I haven't given it much thought at all. Do I *have* to take a date? Can't I just show up?"

Candy replies, "The starting quarterback has to have a date! Ricky, don't you know anything about high school politics?"

"What do *you* know? You've been in high school for all of five seconds," I say.

"I watch *Gossip Girl*," Candy says in her defense.

Hope cracks up. "Girl, bye!"

Candy's little comedy break saved Ricky from having to either commit to a date with Hope or turn her down. Either option would've been all bad, I think. But the look on Hope's face tells me that she hasn't given up on Ricky.

By the time we get to the bowling alley, the party is already popping. There are Longfellow High students all over the place, and students from other schools too.

"Wow, Hope! This party is the bidness!" exclaims Candy.

Hope beams. "It wasn't just me, planning this. It was all of the rally girls working together."

Ricky walks up with several pairs of bowling shoes. "Are y'all ready to get demolished?"

I cover my mouth, but the laughter spills out anyway. "Boy, whatever. Don't let that little football win blow your head up. We're gonna crush him, right, Kev?"

"That's right! Who else is on our team?" Kevin asks.

"Count me in," says Hope. "I really want to beat Ricky now since he's talking mess."

Candy says, "Ricky, I'll be on your team."

"Can you bowl?" he asks.

Candy giggles and slaps Ricky on the arm. "Not really, but I just wanted to help you out."

Ricky throws his arms into the air. "Can I get one decent player on my team?" he asks.

"I'll be on your team, Rick."

Valerie stays sneaking up on somebody. She's standing here with her arms crossed, with Jewel and Kelani at her side.

"Umm, okay, sure. I guess," Ricky says.

Hope looks about ready to explode, which in any other scenario would be quite hilarious to me. But since this is a Valerie-induced anger, I'm going to resist making any jokes that might make this situation worse.

Kevin grabs an empty lane for us and starts filling out the computerized score card. Why does he scribble his own name as "Kev-Dogg" on the screen? Every time I think he's ready to join us in the land of cool, he runs back to the dark side.

Jewel is on our team, and we let Rick's squad have Kelani. Now I think we're pretty even with player talent. Jewel claims she's never bowled before, so she should make up for Ricky's unfortunate Candy situation.

"So, Rick," Valerie says as she slides up next to Ricky on the bench. "It is okay if I follow you to Cedar Point next week, right?"

Ricky clears his throat nervously. "It's a straight shot. You just take Highway Two West the whole way. You can't miss it."

Valerie snuggles up so close to Ricky that there is no

space between them. "But I'd feel so much safer if I followed you. What if we get lost?"

Ricky scoots away from her. "Well, I don't care if you follow us. I'm driving with the people from my church. Be at Gia's house next Saturday morning at nine."

"Let's bowl, people!" Kevin says excitedly. He is *way* too pumped about this game.

Kevin goes first and makes a strike. He does some kind of crazy little move that he calls his victory dance. Umm, yeah, no.

The rest of us take turns throwing balls into the gutter or knocking down one or two pins. Even Ricky is playing horribly, and he's usually pretty good. Maybe he's tired from the football game, but I'm almost one hundred percent sure he's thrown off by all of the booty popping by Valerie and hair-flinging by Hope. Yes, he *does* seem to be a bit distracted by Hope, but I can't tell if he likes or dislikes the attention.

When Valerie knocks down three pins and then drops it like it's hot to celebrate, I guess it's too much for Ricky. He grabs me by the arm and says, "Come on, Gia, let's go get some snacks. Kevin, bowl on our turns, okay?"

Kevin says, "Oh, sure! You just want me to get some points on your sorry boards."

Ricky ignores Kevin's foolishness and drags me toward the refreshment counter. He says, "Gia, what in the world is going on? Why are Hope and Valerie acting all crazy?"

"Boy, quit acting like you don't know. Obviously, they both want to be your boo."

"Well, I guess I knew about Valerie, but Hope? Hope likes me too?" Ricky asks with anxiety in his voice.

"Yep, I guess she couldn't handle all of your hotness."

Ricky sits down at one of the tables and runs his hand over his hair. It's one of his nervous tics. He says, "Gia, Hope can't like me. I mean, I don't think of her in that way."

I swallow hard. It's a good thing I've never let any of my almost-crush feelings get out of control. I mean, this could very easily be me he's talking about.

"So what are you going to do?" I ask.

"Can I pretend that I don't notice? Do you think they'll let me play stupid?"

This is almost too easy. "*Play* stupid? The fact that you are just now noticing this little triangle kinda confirms that you are not playing."

"I am not in the mood for your jokes," Ricky fusses. "I need some help here. You have to get your friends off of my back, especially Hope."

Hmmm . . . especially Hope? Does that mean that there is some chance for Valerie to make it back to boo status? It is my fervent prayer that this is not the case. I have no intentions of dealing with Valerie mixing in with my inner circle of friends.

"So what about Valerie? I think she's pretty much determined to be your date for the Homecoming dance. I hear she's planning to run for Homecoming queen."

"So? What do I have to do with that?" Ricky asks.

"Well, you're pretty popular now, seeing that you're the starting quarterback," I explain.

"I'm not even a senior! Plus, I don't care about any of that Homecoming court mess."

"Hear, hear, my brother!" I say while giving Ricky a high-five. "Who in the world wants to be the Duchess of Longfellow High?"

"I know, right?" Ricky laughs a little bit and seems to relax. "I guess we should go back over there now," he says. He points over to our lane, and both Hope and Valerie are staring in our direction.

I give Ricky a pat on the back and say, "It's gonna be a long day at Cedar Point next Saturday."

★ 13 ★

We're up bright and early for our family adventure to Cedar Point. Ugh! Gwen is in the kitchen packing a picnic basket full of sandwiches, fruit, cookies, and other foods that I will not be eating. The entire point of going to Cedar Point is eating the cheese fries, caramel apples, and ice cream at Pierre's Ice Cream store.

Candy is in front of the mirror appraising her outfit. I have to admit that her House of Deréon jean skirt and baby tee are pretty fresh, but I refuse to give her any compliments on her stolen goods.

I've decided to bring Mr. Tweety out for some air. In honor of our amusement-park trip, I'm wearing my white Tweety polo shirt with a ferris wheel on the front. It may not be high couture, but it is completely felony-activity free.

"You sure you don't want to borrow something of mine?" Candy asks, after looking my outfit up and down.

"No. That's called receiving stolen property."

"Will you lighten up? It's not that serious really."

"Actually, it is that serious, and if you don't simmer down with all of that boosting, I might just have to snitch on you."

Candy glares angrily. "You wouldn't dare."

"Yes, I would. You have absolutely nothing on me, so I really don't mind getting you in trouble."

Candy stares at me intently as if she's trying to see if I'm serious. I'm not. I just like to keep her worried. She is a permanent fixture on my prayer list, though. She needs some deliverance for real.

Gwen pops her head into our bedroom. "Are you girls almost ready? I think your friends are outside."

"Yes! Let's roll, Mama Gwen," Candy says.

Candy is killing me with this Mama Gwen stuff. I'm totally accepting of her getting along with my mom, but I hope they don't think we're starting a trend here. I have no intentions of calling LeRon Dad, Daddy, Papa, Pops, or any of the above.

Gwen raises an eyebrow in Candy's direction. "Girl, you sure do have a lot of clothes. I don't think I've ever seen you repeat an outfit."

I stifle a snicker as Candy's face turns pale with fear. She better not play Mama Gwen too close. Gwen is very, very observant and her "mess" radar stays connected and in place.

Candy replies, "I guess my mother goes a little overboard sometimes on the clothes thing."

"Mmm-hmmm . . ." Gwen says. "You girls make sure to go to the bathroom before we leave. It's a long ride."

Candy and I look at each other and crack up laughing.

What are we, toddlers? Gwen doesn't even note the reason for our laughter because she's off to take care of her man.

I step into the living room and look out the window. Ricky, Hope, and Kevin are here and they're standing outside Ricky's car. Valerie has just pulled up too. I better hurry and get out there before the fireworks start.

But wait a minute. Oh my goodness. I cannot believe Gwen and her husband are trying to destroy my life. They are wearing matching outfits, and trust, it's *all* bad. They have on navy blue shorts and T-shirts that say *What Would Jesus Do?*. But the worst part is the matching neon-green fanny packs.

I expect this kind of foolishness from Kevin, but not Gwen. Clearly Elder LeRon is a bad influence.

"Mom, what are you wearing?" I ask.

"LeRon picked it out. Do you like it? We're twins!"

I shake my head with utter disgust and walk out the front door. I cannot and will not approve of this. She gets a big, fat *no, ma'am!*

"Hey, y'all," I say as I walk over to Ricky's car.

Ricky looks relieved to see me, and I can guess why. Hope and Valerie look like they're about to pounce on him at any second. I've never seen my friend under this kind of stress!

Valerie says, "Ooo-OOO!"

Every Hi-Stepper here replies with the usual, "Ooo-OOO!"

I don't know how necessary our Hi-Stepper bird call is outside of a football setting. It's almost like Valerie wants

Hope to feel like an outsider. That is so the opposite of cool.

"I'm calling shotgun in Ricky's car!" I shout.

Kevin grimaces. "Hey, I already claimed it when he picked me up."

"Umm, that doesn't count because everyone was not present and accounted for."

Ricky laughs. "Yeah, Kev. I think Gia is right."

"Ha!" I say and jump into the front seat of Ricky's car.

Kevin mutters something and climbs into the backseat. Hope doesn't look too thrilled either, but I'm glad I thought of it first.

"Gia, if you're going to sit in the front then you cannot take a nap like you always do!" Ricky says. "This is a long ride and I'm going to need some conversation."

"I got you!" I reply.

"If she falls asleep, you can call me and we can chat all the way there. I'm sure I can keep you awake," Valerie says from her post on the sidewalk.

I was wondering when she was gonna work her way into the conversation. It's not like Valerie to stand off to the side in silence, especially when there's a cute boy to be preyed upon.

A nervous chuckle escapes from Ricky. "Umm . . . I think Gia will stay up. Right, Gi-Gi?"

I hang my head out of the car window. "I said, I got you! Let's roll out!"

Candy finally joins us outside. "Valerie, can I ride with you?" she asks.

"Of course, chica. Hi-Steppers roll deep like that."

Whatever! I am so over this Hi-Steppers united mess. It will do us all a world of good when Valerie gets over it too.

Ricky gets in on his side of the car and brings in his brand-new scent. It smells good, I guess. But I thought he was trying to avoid the ladies. I'm thinking somebody is not being honest.

"So did you get that new Axe body spray, Ricky?" I ask with a giggle.

Ricky grimaces. "It's not Axe body spray. It's Escape for men. I took it off my dad's dresser. Does it stink?"

"No, actually, it does not."

Ricky flashes that heartbreaking smile at me. "Well, I know you would tell me if it did, so I guess I'm safe."

Hope leans up from the backseat and says, "You smell great, Ricky. Don't worry about Gia. She is a full-time hater."

I stretch my arms over my head and *accidentally* bop Hope on her dome. "Oops! You need to sit back anyway. I didn't call shotgun to have your face all up here in our bidness."

Hope rolls her eyes at me and falls back into her spot next to Kevin. Neither of them look happy about the seating arrangement, but oh well.

Once we get on the freeway Ricky asks, "Y'all want to listen to some music?"

"Do you have Mary Mary?" Kevin asks.

Ricky looks in the rearview mirror and smiles. "Of course, Kev. That's what you want to hear?"

"Yes, sir!"

"Wait!" I say. "Before we start the music, I want to ask everyone a question."

"What is it?" Hope asks.

"If one of you knew someone who was breaking the law, on the regular, would you tell on them?" I ask.

Of course I know I'm talking about Candy, but they don't know that. I can see Ricky and Hope's brain gears going on overdrive, trying to figure out who I'm talking about. And Kevin, well, I have absolutely no idea what he's thinking, but he has a totally weird look on his face.

"Breaking the law how?" Ricky asks.

"Shoplifting."

"Ooh! It's Valerie, isn't it?" Hope asks.

"No, it's not Valerie."

Kevin asks, "Do you have proof that this person is shoplifting or is it just a suspicion?"

I nod. "Yes, I have proof."

"So you should tell," says Ricky. "Wait, it's not anyone in this car, right?"

"No!" I say. "It's Candy."

"The blood of Jesus!" shouts Kevin. "We need to go into prayer, right now."

Hope, Ricky, and I give Kevin a moment of silence until he pulls himself together. He just slipped into church-mother mode right then.

"Sorry, y'all," Kevin says as he tries to avert his eyes from mine.

"It's all good, Kevin. But seriously, y'all, what am I gonna do?"

Hope sighs. "Well, if you tell your mom, Candy's gonna get in big trouble, right?"

"Yeah, Elder LeRon will go ballistic."

"Then I say you tell on her," says Ricky. "It's for her own good."

Hope says, "I don't know, Gia. I think you should leave it alone and let God reveal it."

Great. All three of my best friends have different opinions. Kevin thinks we should pray and cast the klepto demon out of her, Ricky says blow the lid off this joint, and Hope says do nothing. Clearly, I need to find a new set of friends strictly for decision-making advice.

Ricky's phone buzzes on the armrest. He reaches for it, but I slap his hand away. "Keep your eyes on the road—I got this," I say.

I pick up the phone and look at the screen. There is a new text message. I look at the screen and read out loud: "'Rick, are you gonna be my partner today? I'm afraid of roller coasters.'"

Hope growls. "Is that from Valerie?"

"Who else?" I ask. "Ricky, should I reply?"

There is terror in Ricky's eyes. "No, Gia. Don't reply. Let me do it."

"No way! You're driving." I start typing on Ricky's keypad. "How's this? 'If you're scared of rides, maybe you should go back home.'"

Hope says, "That sounds good. Send it!"

"Gia, you better not send that," Ricky warns.

"What's going to happen if I do?"

Ricky scowls at me and snatches his phone. With one hand he deletes the text message and puts his phone in his pocket.

"Dang, Ricky. I was just playing," I say innocently. "I wasn't really going to send that."

Hope has a hurt expression on her face. "Wow, Ricky. Do you like Valerie after how she played you last year?"

"No, I don't like her that way. Why do I have to like anyone? Why can't we all just be cool?" Ricky sounds really frustrated with this love triangle scenario.

Hope replies, "It's hard to just be cool with someone if you really like that person in a beyond cool kinda way."

See, why'd she have to go and say that? If it wasn't already uncomfortably awkward in here, it sure is now. Hope has got to see that Ricky is not ready for this action, not to mention that her tirade also applied to me and Kevin. Ugh. I hate to even think *me and Kevin* in a sentence.

Hope has pretty much killed any chance of conversation for the rest of this ride. She and Kevin sleep and snore in the back and I'm playing video games on Ricky's phone while Mary Mary sings on the stereo. Ricky's hands are gripping his steering wheel so tightly that his knuckles are white, and his face is twisted into a distressed frown.

I glance at Ricky out of the corner of my eye and whisper, "You know it's cool what you said. Hope needed to hear that. Valerie does too."

"It's not that I don't like her, Gia. It's just that this whole 'maintaining my virtue' is pretty tough when girls are throwing themselves at me," Ricky whispers back.

I clear my throat and roll my eyes. "Boy, I don't see anyone throwing themselves at you, but I get where you're coming from."

* * *

It's about 10:30 a.m. when we finally arrive at the park. We all pay, using some form of discount ticket (it costs a grip to get in Cedar Point, on the real). Then we split away from Gwen and Elder LeRon. They're going to meet up with the other parents who found it necessary to tag along.

Hope seems sad so I try to cheer her up. I whisper to her, "Now that we know what's up with Ricky, won't it be fun to watch Valerie try to hook up with him?"

She doesn't seem cheered at all. Isn't she the one who claimed to have so much spirit? Wow. I sure don't see it.

The first ride of the day is always a roller coaster called Blue Streak. We ride it first because it is right at the front of the park. Plus, it's pretty tame, unlike the rest of the roller coasters in the park, so the wait is usually under an hour.

While we stand in line, roasting in the early September sun, Valerie squeezes through everyone to stand next to Ricky. Ricky tries not to look annoyed, I think, but he's not doing a great job at all. He looks like he wishes Valerie would disappear.

Valerie sits next to Ricky on the metal railing that keeps the line in order. If he wasn't wearing sunglasses, I'd probably be able to see him rolling his eyes. Valerie doesn't seem to notice anything out of the ordinary.

"Did you get my text, Rick?" she asks.

Ricky nods. "Yeah, I got it, but I was driving so I couldn't respond."

"It's cool. So are we riding together or not?"

"Yes, on this one," Ricky snaps. "But I'd also like to ride with everyone else too. We should switch off."

Valerie laughs. "Sure. You act like I'm about to eat you up or something!"

"Well . . ."

"Ricky! You can't possibly think I'm trying to hook up with you. I'm just teasing with you."

Ricky takes his sunglasses off and his eyes are open wide. They seem to be smiling. He says, "Seriously, Valerie? You're not trying to hook up?"

"No, papi. Not after last year. But I just wanted you to know that I feel totally bad about what I did to you and I apologize. I hope we can be friends."

Ricky says, "Valerie, I forgive you and we can totally be friends! I'd like that."

I almost choke on the soda I've been sipping while watching this little soap opera. Who does Valerie think she's fooling? I can see right through this mess. Ricky, on the other hand, seems pleased. I thought I'd taught him better than this.

Everyone is in harmony for a few hours, but of course, it doesn't last. It is past lunchtime now, and the diehard roller coaster fans (Ricky, Valerie, Candy, and I) want to keep going to our favorite ride—the Millenium Force. But some weak individuals (Jewel, Kelani, Hope, and Kevin) want to find the grown folk and eat barbeque and whatever else they're cooking over in the picnic area.

I say, "Why don't we just split up? The line for Millenium Force is gonna be a good two hours. Y'all can go eat and meet us back here."

Hope protests, "We should all stay together. That's how people get lost. It won't take long for us to get a bite to eat and then come back to the line. Aren't y'all hungry?"

"I'm not!" says Valerie as she pulls Ricky toward the roller coaster.

"Me either," replies Candy, who runs after Valerie and Ricky.

"Hope, you don't even like this ride," I argue. "Just meet us back . . . okay? Text me when you're coming back."

Hope gazes after Ricky with longing in her eyes. I know she doesn't want to leave Ricky alone with Valerie, but it's pretty much a done deal. I jog over to the line to join my fellow roller-coaster fanatics.

I say, "Ricky, we're riding together on this one, okay?"

"Okay!"

Valerie's facial expression tells me that I was right about her *let's be friends* bit being a scam. She looks ready to scratch my eyeballs out.

But instead of trying to do me bodily harm she reaches up and gently takes Ricky's sunglasses off. She puts them on her face and strikes a pose like she's about to throw a football. Ricky grins, but she looks corny as what.

"Is that supposed to be me?" Ricky asks.

Valerie nods. "Do I have you down?"

"Umm, no," I say.

Candy says, "That is totally Ricky, all day and all night."

Valerie puts the sunglasses back on Ricky's face and takes her time doing it. She inhales deeply and closes her eyes, all the while her body is centimeters from grinding on Ricky.

"What are you wearing, Rick? You smell good enough to eat," Valerie says with a little growl.

I guess she's supposed to sound hungry or something. Umm, yeah . . . no.

Ricky shrugs. "It's just something I found on my dad's dresser."

Valerie laughs. "Well, you shouldn't wear that around me if we're going to be just friends."

"I'll keep that in mind."

Oh, good grief! This is so sickening, and I've got a pretty strong stomach.

Candy says, "How long are we going to be standing in one spot? It seems like we've been in line forever already."

"We've been in line for fifteen minutes," Ricky says, glancing down at his watch.

"Well, it feels like forever." Candy's bottom lip protrudes in a pout.

Valerie says, "I know what we can do to pass the time. We can practice our step for next week."

I let out a groan. "No, ma'am. I do not feel like stepping right now."

"Oh come on, Gia!" says Candy. "It'll be fun."

"We don't have any music," I protest.

Valerie and Hope line up in the small space between the metal line dividers. "We don't need music. We've got the beat up here." Valerie points to her temple and starts clapping.

When I still refuse to join them, Valerie and Candy do about half of our step to "No One" by Alicia Keys. They actually look pretty good besides the fact that Valerie keeps *accidentally* flipping one side of her skirt in the air, giving Ricky an unnecessary view of her thigh.

I hear Ricky draw in a sharp breath and hold it. He pushes his sunglasses up on his nose and turns his head away from Valerie. I pat him on the back, acknowledging his struggle. He's doing a lot better than most dudes his age. I'm actually proud of him.

But if Ricky is going to keep associating with Valerie on this *just friends* nonsense, I am immediately placing my best friend on Kevin's prayer list.

★ 14 ★

After spending all day walking around Cedar Point and standing in two-hour-long lines, you would think we would all be tired. But if you thought that, you would be wrong, because now we're chilling in Ricky and Kevin's hotel room at the Sandusky Marriott. We've ordered lots of pizza and the parents have been banished down the hallway to their own rooms.

Of course, Gwen and LeRon have promised to check on us in a couple of hours to make sure that we all are still fully clothed and not committing any sins. I sure do appreciate them for that . . . Not!

Hope is still extra heated with me because we never did hook back up after we split up at the park. We waited for them at the ride, but when they didn't show up, we got cheese fries and kept it moving. Hope claims she tried to call me, but I guess my phone was off.

Anyhoo, she got stuck with Kevin and the giggle twins

for the rest of the day. She should be thanking me, because Kevin won her a giant panda bear at the ring-toss game. That was a serious come-up.

I pat Mister Panda Bear on the head. "Hope, this bear is so cute! Kevin, you must've spent a grip trying to win this."

"Nope," Kevin says, "I won it on the second try. It was supposed to be yours, Gia."

"Bummer!" I say, and then quickly move over to the pizza boxes before his rebuttal.

Valerie announces, "Okay, y'all, it's game time. Who's up for truth or dare?"

This cannot end well. I hate playing these clichéd teenager games. Lemme think . . . I vote no!

Hope beams. "I love truth or dare!"

Next thing you know, we'll be playing that three-minutes-in-the-closet game. As soon as someone tries to force me to stand in a dark closet in close proximity to Kevin, that's where I draw the line. I don't care if he does have contact lenses, the moistness and clamminess have not yet ceased to exist.

We push the two double beds together and everyone sits in a circle. Although I am completely unwilling to be a part of this, how can I not? I'll look like a total lame if I don't participate.

Kelani pulls a name out of Ricky's baseball cap. "Okay, Jewel. You're first. Truth or dare?"

Jewel bites her lip and deliberates for a moment before saying, "Truth."

"Who is the better choreographer on the Hi-Steppers squad? Gia or Valerie?"

I roll my eyes. So it's going to be this kind of evening?

I kind of feel sorry for Jewel, because it's going to be difficult for her to give the correct answer with Valerie staring at her with her nose flared out. And, by the way, if you were wondering, the correct answer is . . . me!

Jewel looks from me to Valerie and swallows hard. She closes her eyes tightly and says in a quiet voice, "Gia."

"Who did you say?" Valerie asks in a menacing voice.

Hope laughs. "She said Gia! Let's keep it moving to the next question."

"No, we're not done with this one," Valerie says angrily. "You think Gia is a better choreographer than me? Kelani, what about you?"

Kelani's eyes widen. "Hey, this wasn't my question. I'm pleading the fifth!"

"Do you feel the same way, Candy?" Valerie asks.

"Umm, Gia is my sister, so I've got to go with her."

Wait a minute. Did we just enter the Twilight Zone? Candy is claiming me as her sister? I wonder if this has anything to do with the fact that I can snitch on her at any time.

"I can't believe this," Valerie says. She snatches the hat from Kelani and picks a name.

"But it's my turn to pick," protests Jewel. She shuts her mouth quickly when Valerie gives her the look of death.

Valerie opens the slip of paper. "Kevin. Truth or dare?"

"Truth. Absolutely, truth," Kevin says. "I have nothing to hide."

Valerie squints. "Hmm . . . is it true that you're jealous of your best friend Ricky?"

Kevin gasps and blinks rapidly like he needs some saline solution for his brand-new contact lenses. I cannot believe

Valerie would ask him something like that. This game is beyond unfriendly.

"I suppose there are some things that I am jealous about. He's a lot smoother than I am, and girls like him," Kevin says. "I don't think I want to play this game anymore."

"I don't either!" I concur.

Hope glares angrily at Valerie and snatches the hat. "No! Why stop now?" She opens the paper. "Valerie. Truth or dare?"

Valerie laughs. "All right. Truth."

"Is it true that you want Ricky to take you to Homecoming just so you'll have a shot at being Homecoming queen?"

Ricky objects. "Hey! Leave me out of this!"

Hope ignores him. "Valerie, answer the question."

"Well, he deserves to go to the dance with the most likely candidate for queen," Valerie says. "Not some busted rally girl who wishes she was me."

Hope stands to her feet. "I don't wish I was you. You are one of the most evil and hateful people I know."

"Who says I'm talking about you? Well, I guess you *are* the only busted rally girl here, so I see how you could think that I was talking about you."

Now they've got me angry, because this was supposed to be a fun outing with my friends, not a bloodbath by Valerie. I do not appreciate this nonsense at all.

"Valerie, I've got a dare for you," I say.

Valerie laughs. "It's someone else's turn."

I reply, "This has nothing to do with this game. I dare you to be a good person. You told me that you'd changed, but I don't see any evidence of that."

Valerie rolls her eyes. "Give me a break, Gia. You didn't say anything to Jewel and Kelani when they asked that stupid choreography question. They're the ones who brought the negativity."

"And you had to continue down the same path, because you got embarrassed?" Ricky asks. "You need to get over yourself, Valerie."

Valerie stands up and walks to the door. "You know what? I'm over all you lames. I'm out of here. Anyone who's in my hotel room better come now, or you aren't getting in."

Jewel and Kelani stand to leave. I say, "Y'all can stay in our room if y'all don't mind sharing a bed. We're not done having fun yet, Valerie. If you want to act evil you can do it by yourself."

Both Kelani and Jewel have a seat back on the bed. Valerie looks undecided. I think she really wants to stay but is too embarrassed to say so. Whatever. I'm definitely not trying to make it easy for her. She hasn't changed one bit. She's still the same mean, sneaky, and conniving Valerie that she's always been.

Ricky says, "Valerie, you're welcome to stay, but only if you're going to be nice."

"Does that rule go for everyone?" Valerie asks.

I guess this is fair, because Hope got a little bit carried away too. I'm just glad they never got around to my turn. I was going to have to say dare, because the questions they were asking were bananas.

"Yes," Ricky says, "it goes for everyone. We're all friends here, so let's keep it friendly."

"Let's play spades!" I suggest. "It's a totally drama–free game."

Valerie's breathing slows and she seems to calm down. She returns to her seat on the bed and says, "Deal me in, Gia."

As I deal the cards I completely change the subject. "So, Ricky, do you think the Spartans are going to go to the state championship this year?"

"Well, we lost in the playoffs last year, but we really want to go all the way this year. I think we've got the squad. Romeo and James have really gotten better this year, and we've got this freshman, Lincoln, who is totally off the chain."

Hearing Romeo's name makes me cringe. I have been doing a good job *not* thinking of that good crush gone bad.

"I know Lincoln!" Candy exclaims. "He is awesome. He was the star running back on our middle school team."

Kelani laughs. "Dang, Candy! Calm down."

"Somebody's got a crush, I think," Jewel teases.

A smile flashes across Candy's face. "Well, he is cute. Unlike some people in this room, I'm not ashamed of my crushes."

Hmm . . . I wonder who she means by "some people"?

★ 15 ★

"Have y'all seen this?" Ricky fusses as he tosses a flyer onto the lunch table where Kevin and I are sitting.

I pick up the flyer and read it. It says, *Ricky Freeman for Homecoming Court*. Fresh from the Cedar Point drama of this past Sunday, Ricky doesn't need this. Ricky is clearly furious, but I feel myself getting slightly amused. We rarely get to see Ricky with attitude, so I'm going to enjoy this.

"So what?" I ask.

"Congratulations!" Kevin says with a smile.

Ricky sits down at the table and crosses his arms angrily. "I did not want to run for Homecoming court. That's not me. I don't even know why someone would nominate me."

"You should take it as a compliment," I say. "Someone thought you were fresh enough to nominate. Deal with it."

"Yeah, you should be proud. No one nominated me," Kevin says.

"Y'all are not getting it. I just want to play football," Ricky explains. "I don't want to be popular because I don't want to date girls, and everybody expects it."

"Why don't you want to go out with anyone, Ricky?" I ask. "You don't have to lose your virtue just because you go out on a date."

Ricky sighs. "Remember what happened with you and Romeo at the lake?"

I want to strangle him for bringing that up. How could I not remember? I'd pay someone hard-earned money to be able to forget that foolishness. Romeo took me out to the lake, tried to make me get busy with him, and then left me there. I'll probably never forget that for as long as I live. Ugh!

"Yes, Ricky," I reply. "Of course I remember."

"Well, some girls are just like Romeo, Gia. They don't stop until you do something freaky with them. Or worse, they accuse you of not liking girls if you refuse."

Dang. I never knew Ricky was under so much pressure. I mean, I've never even considered that boys have to worry about their reputations too. No wonder Ricky wants to stay completely low-key.

"Ricky, how about if you, me, and Kevin all go to Homecoming together, like a crew?" I suggest. "Then you won't feel obligated to have a date."

"That sounds good. But will I say I already have a date if someone asks?"

I pause for a moment to think. Then the answer comes to me. "You should just say that you have plans."

"Okay, enough about Ricky's nonissues! Can we work on our assignment?" Kevin asks.

"What do we have written down so far?" Kevin and I have been working on our story line while we waited for Ricky to arrive.

Kevin clears his throat and reads, "Well, we have the main character as a guy named Steve who has superpowers. He's telepathic and he sees into the mind of a girl named Helena. Helena likes him but acts mean to him every opportunity she gets. But he doesn't give up because he knows she likes him, because he can read her mind."

Ricky blinks rapidly. "Are y'all serious?"

"Yeah! You don't think that's good?" I ask.

Ricky replies, "Umm . . . it sounds like y'all watch too many shows on the Sci-Fi Network."

Okay, so that is one thing that Kevin and I do have in common. Science fiction is the bidness for real. Ricky is a total lame for *not* liking sci-fi.

Kevin asks, "Do you have something better?"

"No. I haven't really thought about it at all," Ricky says with a shrug.

"Then we're going with me and Kevin's story line," I reply.

"Okay, cool. But as soon as y'all put Simon in some tights . . ."

"His name is Steve," Kevin says indignantly.

Ricky rolls his eyes. "Whatever, dude! As soon as y'all put *Steve* in some tights and a cape, I'm asking Ms. Beckman to change my group."

"You can't change! You're stuck with us," I declare while trying to restrain a giggle.

Valerie and her brand-new mini-me, Candy, sashay up to the lunch table. Candy has totally and unapologetically jacked Valerie's swag. She's wearing her long hair straight like Valerie's and clipped on the side with a barrette. Of course, she's rocking some stolen goods—a pair of Lucky jeans and a top that she got from Express. The most shocking part of Candy's hookup is the Louis Vuitton bag that is most definitely out of her budget.

"Wow, Candy," Kevin says, "you look like a model."

Valerie smiles. "She does, doesn't she?"

"Thank you, Kevin," Candy replies with a tight, Valerie-like smile.

I lift an eyebrow angrily and say, "Nice bag, Candy."

"Do you like it?" she says. "I got it on sale."

"It must've been some sale," I continue, "seeing that your allowance is only twenty dollars a week."

Valerie scrunches her nose distastefully. "Don't be a hater, Gia. It's not a good look."

"Whatever!" I roll my eyes and chomp one of Kevin's French fries.

Valerie picks up one of Ricky's flyers from the table. "Rick! You're running for Homecoming court?"

"Unfortunately."

Valerie grins. "I didn't think you'd put your name in."

"I didn't," Ricky replies.

"Well, it's still hot!" Candy exclaims. "Valerie's gonna be the queen and you're going to be one of the princes!"

"Pump your brakes, chica. We don't want to jinx it."

"I'm sorry, Valerie."

Valerie pats Candy on the back. "It's all good."

Should I be annoyed that Candy has adopted herself a new big sister? Lemme think. Umm . . . that's a negative.

Valerie says, "Come on, girl. I'm hungry for salad."

Riddle me this. Who is ever hungry for salad? I've been hungry for pizza, hamburgers, spaghetti, and even a good piece of birthday cake. But I have never, ever been hungry for salad. Valerie is weird.

Kevin's eyes follow Candy and Valerie as they glide across the cafeteria. Yes, glide. Valerie moves like that on purpose so that people will stop what they're doing and look at her.

And of course Candy's gliding because Valerie is gliding. Boo!

Kevin takes a sip of his apple juice and swallows hard. "Gia, your little sister is cute."

"Get real, Kevin," I say. "She's a criminal."

Ricky laughs. "Are you jealous, Gia?"

Without thinking, my fist lodges itself in Ricky's arm. "Ow!" he yelps in between laughs.

Kevin gushes, "I'm sorry, Gia. She's nothing compared to you."

"Shut up, Kevin," I reply.

"But Gia, I mean it. You are a beautiful flower . . ."

"Ugh! I mean it, Kevin," I warn.

Ricky clutches his stomach from laughing so hard. "Kev, man. Quit it, before she swings on you."

"Listen to the man," I concur.

"Did you tell your mom about her shoplifting?" Ricky asks after finally calming his laughter to a dull roar.

"Not yet. There hasn't been a good time," I admit.

"Well," Ricky says, "you better hurry, because it looks like she's not planning to quit anytime soon."

I look across the cafeteria at Candy and I watch her mimic Valerie. Right down to the way Valerie throws her head back in laughter, Candy is a carbon copy. It suddenly occurs to me that last school year Hope was Candy. Hope found out the hard way about how quickly Valerie loses interest in her friends.

I wonder how long it will take for Candy to find out.

★ 16 ★

Gwen holds a piece of paper close to her nose and reads it slowly. What's written on the paper scares me worse than one of those Japanese horror movies. What is this terrifying piece of printed material?

It is a recipe.

The Lord cannot possibly be pleased.

Gwen hands me her vegetable chopper and says, "Gia, chop up this onion for me. I need a chopped onion and green pepper."

I take the small, plastic appliance from her hand and put half an onion inside. She's attempting to make Elder LeRon's favorite dish—jambalaya and corn bread. I suppose she's figured out that this new husband of hers is not going to eat baked chicken and spaghetti every day of the week.

"Maybe we should've started with something easier," I say as Gwen looks in the cupboard for spices.

"You don't think I can do this, Gia?"

"Umm . . ."

"Seriously, Gia? Any idiot can follow a recipe."

I know she doesn't *really* want me to respond to that. I have seen many recipes bite the dust at the hands of Sister Gwen. I remember a bowl of spinach dip that poisoned the entire singles' ministry like it was one of the ten plagues of Egypt.

"So why are you cooking all this anyway, Mom? Is it a special occasion?"

"No. I just want to make sure LeRon is happy. It's part of my ministry as a wife."

Are you kidding me? I think I just heard a bunch of little violins start playing. When she was single, Gwen never seemed to have a ministry of motherhood. I ate cereal so many nights that my body was shocked to have a piece of meat instead of a Cheerio.

Now all of a sudden, cooking is part of her ministry. Boo, Gwen! Just boo!

I've been trying to think of a way to bring up Candy's little problem without being an obvious snitch. But nothing has opened up conversation-wise that would allow me to do this. So, I guess I'm going to just have to do the necessary.

"Mom, I have something to tell you . . ."

Gwen looks alarmed. "What? What is it?"

"First, you have to promise not to say anything."

"I will not promise anything. What have you done?"

"I haven't done a thing, but it's not my business to tell, so maybe I'll just keep it to myself."

Gwen sighs. "Gia, I cannot promise not to say anything. But I will promise that I won't say anything unless it's absolutely necessary."

I consider this for a moment. Gwen may not think that it's necessary to tell LeRon about Candy. As a matter of fact, she just might handle it herself. Not that this will be any easier for Candy, but it might be easier on me.

"Well, Candy . . . she steals."

Gwen's mouth falls open. "What do you mean, 'she steals'? What does she steal? Money from my purse? From her daddy's wallet? What?"

I should've prepared myself for Gwen's rapid-fire inter-rogation style. Good grief! The president should hire her for terrorist questioning, because she is ridiculous with this!

"No, Mom, it's not like that. She steals stuff from stores."

"She shoplifts?"

"Yes, but it's not just little stuff. She takes hundred-dollar jeans and Louis Vuitton purses."

Gwen sits down on the barstool and fans herself with the recipe. "So that's where she's been getting all those fancy outfits?"

"Yes."

"Have you actually seen her do it? Were you with her?"

"No, I've never seen it, but she's pretty much admitted to it and said that her dad wouldn't believe it if I told on her."

Gwen takes the green pepper and slices it with a knife. I should say she's murdering the poor vegetable. I know she's thinking about what to say to Miss Candy when she walks in the house.

But I've done my part. My work is done. Let Jesus take the wheel.

Right after we get Gwen's pot of jambalaya surprise (it'll be a surprise if we can actually eat it) into the pot, Candy opens the front door, looking runway ready. Earlier, I didn't notice her shoes. This child has the audacity to be wearing the black patent leather Juicy Couture pumps that I saw on sale at TJ Maxx.

"Candy, get yourself in here, right now," Gwen says. Dang, she didn't even let her get in the door good.

"Yes, Mama Gwen? Is there something wrong?" Candy asks as she sits on one of the barstools.

"I was going through your laundry and I noticed something strange," Gwen says.

Candy's eyes widen and she moves her Louis Vuitton off of the counter. Too late, boo. Gwen already peeped that out.

"What did you notice?"

"Well, you have several pairs of designer jeans that look brand-new. I also saw various expensive underwear that I know your father did not buy and I *hope* your mama didn't buy. Do you care to explain?"

Candy rolls her eyes. "Is that all? I used my Christmas and birthday money to go shopping, Mama Gwen. My grandparents really hook me up during the holidays. Plus, some of those jeans belong to my friend."

Gwen narrows her eyes, probably fine-tuning the mess radar. Candy smiles confidently and doesn't look away for a second. This seems to put Gwen off, because she loves to do her little stare-downs. She uses the stare-downs to catch me in lies, and she does it well.

I've got to admit, Candy is hardcore. She's got this down to a science, for real.

Gwen says, "All right, girl. I just want you to know that I'm watching you. I'm not going to have any foolishness going on up in here. You better believe that."

"I know you're watching me," Candy says sweetly. "And the good Lord Jesus is watching us all."

Oh no she didn't. If you see the sky cracking, please let me know so I can avoid the lightning! I'm taking myself right into our bedroom, because if the Lord doesn't bring the pain, Mama Gwen just might.

Unfortunately Candy is right behind me. She slams the door and stands in front of my bed where I'm chillaxin' with Mr. Tweety.

"You are such a hater, Gia."

"Um, what?"

"I know you snitched to your mother, and that's foul. Valerie warned me about your hateration."

I would say something, but it's against my religion to respond to foolishness.

Candy continues, "You're just mad, 'cause your clothes are wack! And your friends are lame! And *you're* lame!"

Candy's chest heaves up and down and little beads of sweat pop out on her forehead. Yeah, she's just a little bit extra right now. Looking crazy.

"Are you done?" I ask.

"Ooooh! I can't stand you, Gia."

"Ditto!"

Candy goes into her closet and pulls out a Juicy warmup suit and lays it across the desk. "This is going to look so *hot* tomorrow. What are you wearing, Gia? Oh, wait, don't even answer that. I already know it's gonna be something from the JCPenney's kids section!"

This heifer starts for real giggling like she's said something funny. Um, yeah . . . no. I'll let her enjoy her foolishness for now. It's only a matter of time before I'm the one tee-hee-hee'ing.

★ 17 ★

"Come on, Gia. Move your butt!" Mrs. Vaughn yells across the gymnasium.

I am late for Hi-Steppers practice today because Kevin wanted to get some work in on our short story. We have a difference of opinion on the ending. I think that our lead female, Helena, should find out Steve can read minds, be freaked out, and run off screaming. Kevin says that's not romantic—as if he would know. But anyway, he wants Helena and Steve to get beyond their differences and attend the senior prom together. I vote no. Kevin can go ahead with all those rainbows, unicorns, and happy endings.

But anyway, our argument has me totally late for practice. Valerie and I have choreographed a sweet step to Kanye West's song "Touch the Sky" and she's already standing in front of the Hi-Steppers teaching it. There is this cross-over move that we do right before we throw our hands up in the sky that is *bananas*! I can't wait to do it at the game on Friday.

The rest of the step is pretty simple stuff, and the Hi-Steppers catch on quickly. Throughout the entire practice, Candy keeps giving me the I-know-you-snitched side eye. Whatever!

At the end of practice, Valerie stands in front of us all. She announces, "I am running for Homecoming queen. All Hi-Steppers are expected to help me be crowned by wearing buttons and passing out flyers."

I cover my mouth and pretend to cough, but I'm really laughing. She's got me messed up if she thinks I'm going to be handing out buttons that say *Be a pal, Vote for Val.* No, ma'am. Absolutely not.

Valerie continues, "Susan Chiang, one of the rally girls, is running against me as queen. As a show of solidarity, we will not be attending any rally girl–sponsored events until after Homecoming, which is three weeks away."

"When you say *we,* who exactly do you mean?" I ask.

The rally girls' bowling party was the hotness! This week they're doing the party at FunNStuff, an arcade and laser-tag spot where everybody hangs. I fully intend to be there, so I don't know what kind of punishment Valerie is gonna have for me.

"I mean *all* of us, Gia. Hi-Steppers stick together."

I hate being torn like this. Trust and believe, I'm down for the Hi-Steppers. I *love* being a Hi-Stepper! But Hope is my cousin and one of my best friends. It doesn't matter to me if she's a rally girl.

"Listen, Valerie, I'll help you become the Homecoming queen, but it won't be by hating on the rally girls."

Mrs. Vaughn dismisses our practice and we all rush to the locker room. I would like to avoid Valerie because I do not want to continue that Hi-Steppers united foolishness. But I brace myself for drama because Kelani, Jewel, Candy, and Valerie are all giving me dirty looks.

I quickly shower and get dressed, not just because I want to get away from this negative air, but because I have to go do a few things for Mother Cranford. I have been seriously neglecting my only source of income. I will be in a straight economic recession if she decides she wants to bless another member of the youth ministry at our church with employment.

Just when I think I'm going to escape without any ridiculous conversations, Valerie blocks my path. The other Hi-Steppers have made a small semicircle around Valerie, so I guess this means they have her back. Whatev!

"Gia, are you sure you want to be a Hi-Stepper?" Valerie asks.

I puff out my cheeks with air. Does this girl know that she sounds like a CD with a scratch on it? Just repeating the same things over and over and over again. She should be tired of hearing herself!

"I didn't join the Hi-Steppers for all this drama, Valerie."

Valerie smirks. "I'm just asking because ever since Hope quit the squad, you don't seem to be one hundred percent with us."

Okay, it's time to end this. I drop my gym bag on the bench and put both hands on my imaginary hips, tilt my head to the side, and narrow my eyes like I most definitely mean business.

"Listen here, chica. You are *not* going to run me off the squad with all your bully tactics. I'm not Hope, sweetie."

"Who's trying to run you off the squad?" Valerie asks.

Candy says, "Better be careful, Valerie. She'll go to Mrs. Vaughn. Snitching seems to be her thing these days."

"Whatever, Candy!"

Valerie pats Candy's arm and says, "It's all right, Candy. I haven't forgotten what you told me about Gia snitching. Although it isn't cool for her to tell on you, we're going to have to discuss your little *problem*. There is no place on this squad for potential felons."

Candy looks as if Valerie just punched her in the stomach. *Potential felon?* Wow! That is too funny. I couldn't have done that better myself. But that's what Candy gets for trying to be all up in my business.

Valerie says, "Anyway, Gia, back to you. If this has anything to do with you and your cousin both being in love with Rick . . ."

"What?" I ask.

"Everyone can see it, Gia. You both drool over him like he's a Krispy Kreme glazed donut."

Wait a minute. While I do love Krispy Kreme donuts, I don't see what their sweet, yummy goodness has to do with Ricky or Hope. I need Valerie to repeat that analogy, because she completely lost me at "donut." Maybe I'm just hungry.

"But you can both have him," Valerie says. "I have decided that I'm no longer interested. His time has run out. I've given him plenty of opportunities to hook up with me, but he's chosen to miss the best thing that could ever happen to him."

Valerie is such a Kanye. She is her own hype man, and the look is not a good one.

I glance up at the clock and it's a quarter till five. I've got to get out. "Valerie, I'm sure Ricky will be happy to hear that. I think he was wondering when you were gonna catch the hint that he doesn't want you."

"How could he not want me?" Valerie asks. "If he likes females, then he would want me. Every boy in this school wants me."

I can't keep my chuckle on the inside. "I know. And more than half of the boys in this school have *had* you. I think Ricky would prefer someone with a little less mileage."

Valerie fumes. "Keep playing, Gia, and you're gonna end up off the squad."

I walk out of the locker room and away from a dozen pairs of eyes. On my way out, I toss my hand in the air and give them all a silent *whatever*.

Hopefully, Valerie is serious about being done with Ricky, because I'm ready to move to the next episode. That whole back-and-forth, broke-down romance was not the business at all!

Speaking of Ricky, he's waiting outside in the school parking lot to drive me to Mother Cranford's house. I was hoping he didn't leave me, because her house is a twenty-minute walk from here. And yes, I could take the bus, but that would require me to part ways with some of my money. I'd rather use up Ricky's gas.

I jump in his car on the passenger side. "What's up, Ricky Ricardo?"

"You're in a good mood!" he says, probably referring to the post-nuke glow I have from destroying Valerie.

"I *am* in a good mood, and you should be too. Valerie just announced to all of the Hi-Steppers that she is over you."

Ricky shrugs. "I thought she already was. She hasn't spoken to me since we all went to Cedar Point. I heard she's going to Homecoming with Romeo."

"Aren't there any seniors that want to go with her?" I ask. "She stays trying to hook up with someone in the junior class. I can't wait until she graduates."

And yes, I am just a tad bit irritated that she's going to Homecoming with my former crush. It's so funny how that Hi-Stepper loyalty only applies when Valerie can use it to her own advantage. It's also funny how the entire squad (except me) falls for it every time.

So not the business.

When we pull up to Mother Cranford's house, Hope is there, standing on the porch. I know Mother Cranford must get sick of us teenagers using her house as the hangout spot. But I'm glad Hope and Ricky are here because it makes the time go by faster and they help!

When Ricky doesn't turn the car off, I ask, "Aren't you staying?"

He glances up at Hope and says, "Nah, I think I'll go hang out with Kevin, and maybe try to finish our paper."

"Is it because of Hope?" I ask.

Ricky sighs. "Kinda. I mean it's weird because I know she likes me. But I can't just avoid her like Valerie! Hope is my people, you know?"

"Yeah, it's just like with me and Kevin. I just keep hoping that one day he'll decide he doesn't like me anymore."

"Now that you put it that way, I understand why you don't want to be around Kev sometimes."

I get out of the car and slam the door. As Ricky backs out of the driveway, I can see Hope's smile fade.

"Hey, Hope. Why didn't you just wait inside?"

She replies, "Because Mother Cranford is your friend, not mine!"

"She's gonna hear you. You know she has supersonic hearing."

From inside her house, Mother Cranford says, "Gia? Is that you? Come on in here!"

I grab Mother Cranford's house key from underneath her potted plant. Hope and I march in and go straight into the kitchen. First order of business is Mother Cranford's afternoon snack, and then my favorite—cleaning the bathroom!

"Mother Cranford, what do you do on the days I don't come by?" I ask.

She replies, "I get it myself. But since I'm paying you, today I can rest my legs."

"Mother, are you in there getting smart?" Hope asks.

"Baby, I have earned the right to get smart. That's what old folk do."

"Well, I wouldn't get too sassy if I were you!" I say. "You don't have your snack yet."

Mother Cranford's response is to turn up the volume on her television. She is not pressed, okay?

"So why didn't Ricky stay?" Hope asks as she opens the freezer and hands me Mother Cranford's favorite— Lean Cuisine.

"He was going to hang out with Kevin, I think."

"Oh."

Dang, I hate how sad Hope sounds. Maybe this will cheer her up. "Valerie says that she's over Ricky."

"Really? I wonder why."

"I think that Ricky was making her look foolish. She's been stalking him since last year and he still won't holla at her."

"Well, he was digging her at first."

"He was. But then she played him like a dummy, so he moved on."

Hope opens her purse and hands me a thick stack of papers. "What is this?" I ask.

"It's a letter that I've written for Ricky. Can you read it and tell me what you think?"

I look down at the pile of at least ten pages covered on the front and back with Hope's curly handwriting in purple ink. Then I look back at my cousin. She has truly lost her mind.

"Do not give him this, Hope."

"But I want him to know how I feel! I have to get this off my chest."

How do I explain this to her without hurting her feelings? "Hope, my mother always says that you should let the boy make the first move."

"I know. My mom says the same thing, but Ricky is taking way too long. It's been like forever."

"Maybe he's not planning to make a move at all," I say.

She counters. "Maybe he's shy."

You've got to be kidding me. When in the world did she get to be so dense?

Hope laughs and says, "Okay, so Ricky is like the

hottest guy in the school. I know he's not shy. I think he won't make a move because my father is the pastor. That is so irritating."

"That might be true, Hope, but just promise me that you will not give him that letter."

"Since you think it's a bad idea, maybe I'll wait, but if he doesn't do or say something soon, I'm going to have to take drastic measures."

I want to just come out and say that Ricky isn't feeling Hope, but is it my place to do that? I'm thinking no. But real talk, somebody's gonna have to tell somebody something, because I'm not feeling this whole getting-stressed-over-other-people's-love-lives. Ugh!

★ 18 ★

Okay, our dinners are already stressful enough with Gwen's interesting culinary creations, so I don't need to have my stepfather and klepto stepsister staring me down. I don't even think I want to know why they're looking all crazy.

LeRon takes a bite of his Mexican cornbread and grimaces. I almost burst into laughter at the expression on his face. He's the one who told Gwen that he wanted variety. I blame him and his complex taste buds.

LeRon clears his throat and says, "Gwen, Candy came to me in tears about something you said to her, and I think we should discuss it as a family."

"Oh really?" Gwen asks. "What has Miss Candy been crying about?"

Candy looks terrified and rightfully so. She must think her daddy is some kind of superhero if she snitched to him on Gwen. My mother's nose is already flaring in and out and that is phase number one of crouching-tiger-hidden-Gwen mode.

"Well, it seems that you've asked her where she got some of her clothing items, as if she'd stolen them," LeRon says. "She felt like you invaded her privacy."

"Is that a fact?" Gwen asks. Now her chest is heaving up and down with rapid, shallow breaths.

"Yes," LeRon says, "but I'd like to get your side of the story. Did it happen this way?"

"*My* side of the story? You want *my* side of the story?"

Aw, man. It's on and popping now. She's repeating herself and her voice has gone up to the next octave. This is not a good thing. If I was LeRon I would stop now while there's still time.

LeRon replies, "Yes, of course. You're my wife, so I definitely want to hear what you have to say."

"Well, that's good to know," Gwen says, "but I am not about to sit up here and defend myself or my parenting skills, especially in front of this child."

LeRon replies, "I understand. Why don't we step into our bedroom and discuss this further?"

"That's what you should've asked from the get-go," Gwen says. "But right now, I'm going to finish my dinner. After I'm done, we can go and discuss this as husband and wife."

I can feel Candy's legs shaking underneath the table, and it makes me want to crack up. That's what she gets. There is no way she's gonna pull that daddy's-little-girl stuff up in here. Gwen isn't having it. At all.

"May I please be excused?" Candy asks with a desperate tone in her voice.

"Yes . . ." LeRon starts.

"No, you may not," Gwen interjects. "You may be excused when you're done eating. From where I'm sitting, it looks like you've hardly touched your Mexican cornbread."

Ooh! Gwen is foul for that. *She* hasn't even touched her Mexican corn slop, and she's the one who made it!

Candy stuffs another forkful of food into her mouth. If I wasn't afraid of Gwen's kung-fu grip I'd be ROFL right now.

Gwen takes a sip of her sweet tea and stands from the table. "LeRon, I'll be in the bedroom whenever you're ready to talk."

All three of us watch Gwen do her angry sashay to the bedroom. Candy's eyes are filled with fear even though LeRon reaches across the table, pats her on the hand and says, "It's going to be all right."

LeRon follows Gwen into their bedroom and closes the door, shutting us out of the very likely argument that's about to go down. Dang! We never get to see the juicy stuff.

Candy and I remain at the table. "Do you think I can throw this out now?" she asks, pointing to her food.

"I don't know, can you?"

Candy narrows her eyes and marches toward the kitchen. When she hears how loud her steps are, she switches to a tiptoe.

After hiding her food in the kitchen garbage can, Candy comes back to the table and whispers, "Why did you throw me under the bus, Gia?"

"What bus? Girl, what are you talking about?"

"You told Gwen all about my boosting, didn't you? Just admit it, Gia."

"I don't know. Did I?"

Candy growls and says, "I *know* you told, Gia. I just don't understand why."

"If I told, and I'm not saying I did, but *if* I told, maybe it was because I don't want you to get in trouble. Too bad I can't say as much for your friends."

"How many times do I have to tell you that I won't get in trouble? It's easy, and it's not hurting anyone."

"God doesn't like stealing," I say.

"God doesn't like haters."

I just roll my eyes and take a swig of my sweet tea. I'm done trying to convince Candy to act like she has some sense. It's only a matter of time before Gwen has proof of what Candy is doing.

Gwen and LeRon come out of their bedroom after a very long and intense few minutes. From the look of disgust I see on Gwen's face, I know that this is far from over. LeRon's arms are crossed tightly across his chest and his eyebrows are dipped low.

Gwen says, "Candy, if you ever feel that you've been treated unfairly, I don't want you to be afraid to come and talk to me. By the same token, if I see something wrong or something that concerns me I'm going to address it."

"Yes, ma'am," Candy replies.

Umm, is somebody going to address how LeRon treats me? Nobody seems to be concerned about how I feel! No one asked me if I wanted this sticky-fingers girl to be joined at the hip with me.

"And another thing, teenagers don't have privacy in

this home," Gwen says. "You can have privacy when you're paying your own bills."

Candy nods in agreement.

Gwen says, "I can't hear you."

"Yes, ma'am," Candy repeats.

Gwen exhales and smiles. "So everything is settled. I'm glad we had this conversation."

Excuse me, what? Nothing is settled! Candy is still determined to be a criminal and LeRon still thinks I'm the problem. But since my mom has had enough excitement for one evening, what with the Mexican surprise (as in surprise, this is *not* cornbread) and Candy's tattling, I'm going to leave it alone.

But this is soooooo not settled.

★ 19 ★

"**G**ia, are you coming tonight?" Hope asks. She's referring to the rally girls' party after the football game.

"I am absolutely there," I reply.

"Good, because I heard that the Hi-Steppers were banned from coming. I thought if that was true that it would just be crazy."

I sigh, stuff my math book into my backpack and slam the door to my locker. "She did tell all of the Hi-Steppers not to come to the party, but no one was banned."

"Why would she do that? What's her problem anyway?"

"She's mad about Susan running for Homecoming queen."

"Are you kidding me? Did she think that they were just going to hand her the crown?" Hope asks.

"I don't know. But I'm so tired of talking about Homecoming. Since when did *my* life revolve around Home-coming?"

"Here comes your boy," Hope says with a grin.

I don't even have to ask who she's talking about be-cause I hear his smooth voice before I even turn around. It's my blast from last year, Romeo. I've been doing a good job of avoiding him so far this school year. We don't have any classes together so it hasn't been that hard.

Why is he staring at me? Wait, let me just say that today, I do look extra fly. Gwen braided the front of my hair to one side and the back is flowing free. It's my favorite style. It looks like Romeo is also appreciating Gwen's hair-styling talents.

"What's up, lil' mama?" Romeo asks.

I look to the left and to the right. "I know you're not talking to me," I say while Hope chuckles.

Romeo replies, "Don't be like that, shorty. You're looking real fresh today, and I just wanted to tell you that Romeo digs it."

"Your admiration is an unfortunate byproduct of my fabulosity."

"Huh?" he asks with a blank stare.

Remind me to ask the Lord why he wasted all that fine-ness on someone with half a brain. But I am dead wrong. I used all of those extra syllables on purpose because I knew that Romeo would be completely clueless.

Romeo and his crew move on down the hallway al-most as if they're one person. Romeo and his flock of mini-Romeos. That's just weird.

Hope looks at me and we both burst into laughter. "I can't believe you liked him," she says.

"I know, right? He is ugh!"

"He doesn't have a thing on my boo Ricky," Hope remarks.

I roll my eyes yet again. My eyeball sockets are going to go on strike from sheer exhaustion. Between Hope, Valerie, and Candy's foolishness, they don't get much of a break.

My cousin and I start walking toward class. I hope that she doesn't want to start talking about that epic novel of a letter that she wrote to Ricky. Maybe she came to her senses and burned the thing.

Valerie, Kelani, and Jewel are walking down the other side of the hallway handing out flyers, which I'm sure are Valerie's Homecoming court propaganda, because she is dead set on winning this thing. That poor Susan better watch her back. I don't put anything past Valerie.

"Ooo-OOO! Good morning, Hi-Stepper!" Valerie says.

This girl has multiple personalities for real. Does she not remember threatening to have me thrown off the squad? And now she's Ooo-OOOing me like it never happened at all.

Valerie grabs my arm and pulls me away from Hope. "I need to borrow your cousin for a second," she says.

"What's up, Valerie?" I ask after shrugging my arm away.

"Two things. First, I'm having a pre-Homecoming hayride Saturday night. Everyone's invited."

"Even Ricky and Hope?"

Valerie smiles sweetly. "Of course they're invited."

"Okay, when does Ashton Kutcher jump out from behind a locker?" I so feel like this is a *Punk'd* episode.

"I told you I was over Rick. I'm actually going to Homecoming with Romeo. Go figure!"

"Go figure," I reply. Yet another cardinal Hi-Stepper rule broken by Valerie.

"It's not like you and Romeo actually dated. I mean, you two didn't hook up or anything . . . did you?"

"Eww! No. You know better than that, Valerie."

Valerie throws her head back and laughs. "You're right. I did know that. But come to the hayride, okay?"

"Are you coming to the rally girls' get-together tonight?"

"I sure am. I have lots of campaigning to do."

This is a surprise. "Okay then, Valerie. We'll be there."

When I rejoin Hope she's got a strange expression on her face. "What?" I ask.

"That was weird. What did Valerie want?"

"To invite us to a hayride tomorrow night."

Hope laughs. "Yeah, right."

"No, seriously. I know it sounds strange, but just roll with it. Valerie throws the bomb parties."

"Will Gwen let you go?" Hope asks. This is a very valid question.

"She'll let me go as long as you're going."

"That's the same thing my dad says. He lets me go if *you're* going."

"Well then, we're covered."

At lunch I tell Ricky and Kevin about Valerie's hayride. I'm greeted with mixed reactions.

"I am not going to any party that Valerie's throwing. I don't even know why you asked," Ricky says.

Kevin says, "It sounds like fun, I'm down."

Ricky and I stare at Kevin in shock. Actually it feels like I'm inside of a crazy body-swap science experiment. Someone put my boy Ricky in Kevin's body.

"What?" Kevin asks. "I like hayrides."

"Since when?" I ask.

Kevin replies, "Since always. Just because I don't ever get invited doesn't mean that I don't like them."

"So you want to go to *Valerie's* hayride?" Ricky asks.

"Sure. There will be cheerleaders, Hi-Steppers, and rally girls, right?"

I shrug. "Probably."

"Well, then I'm there!" Kevin exclaims and takes a huge bite out of his tuna sandwich.

First and foremost, I don't know if I can get used to a Kevin who wants to chase any girls other than me. Second, I will not be held responsible for any catastrophies that occur from a hormone-crazed Kevin running wild. Lastly, someone should really tell Kevin that hot boys don't eat tuna sandwiches for lunch. I'm just saying.

"If Kevin's going, you can't not go," I say to Ricky.

"If I go, I'm not talking to Valerie at all," he responds.

"I'm sure she won't mind since her man, Romeo, is gonna be there."

Ricky's eyebrows go up in surprise. "Romeo? Valerie's dating Romeo now?"

"Well, I know they're going to Homecoming together."

Ricky asks, "Are you cool with that?"

"Of course!" I exclaim. "I been over that dude. She can run off and marry him if she wants. I'm done."

"Speaking of Homecoming, how's your campaign going, Ricky?" Kevin asks. "Do you need me to hand out any flyers?"

Ricky scowls at Kevin. "Why would I be campaigning? I didn't submit my name."

"No one is stopping you from withdrawing," I remark.

"I thought about it," Ricky says, "but then whoever nominated me might be upset."

Now Ricky is getting the blank stare. Who does he think he's fooling? I think Ricky wants to be Homecoming prince, but he doesn't want us to know he wants it. Was that too much? I'll wait while you reread that sentence.

"Okay, Ricky," I say. "We believe you. Right, Kevin?"

Kevin winks at me. "Right!"

Ricky clenches his teeth and rolls his eyes. "Whatever to both of y'all."

★ 20 ★

Tonight, the Longfellow Spartans are facing their worst rival—the Euclid Heights Titans. Euclid Heights has three All-American players on their offensive line and two on the defensive squad. In a word, they are beasts.

They've already sacked Ricky once, and we're only in the first quarter. Romeo, who plays tailback, is struggling to gain any yardage on the passes that he does catch. I know they're glad that this isn't Homecoming week.

"All right, Hi-Steppers!" yells Valerie from her place in the stands. "It's time for us to pump our team up."

Isn't this supposed to be the cheerleaders' job? Not that I'm against school spirit or anything, but dang, can we stay in our own lane?

Then I see the rally girls out of the corner of my eye. They have a bunch of red and white flags that they're waving as they chant, "Spartans fight! Spartans fight!"

Valerie starts a one-two step with the Hi-Steppers, who are now standing. The one-two step . . . one-two step, goes in time with the rally girls' chant.

As we do our impromptu step, people in the stands join in by stomping out, or clapping out, the one-two step. It actually sounds kind of hot!

All of the chanting, stepping, clapping, and stomping seems to help the team on the field. In the second quarter, James, a defensive back, intercepts a pass from the Titans quarterback and returns it for a touchdown. The crowd, of course, goes wild.

We are still pumped as we run onto the field for the halftime show. We totally rock that Kanye West song, and even have the crowd throwing their hands up in the air with us. We don't do solos, because Mrs. Vaughn doesn't care for any one person trying to hog the spotlight, but Valerie always does something extra that wasn't planned in the choreography. This time she does a little Beyoncé booty bounce on her way off the field and the boys cheer like they've lost their minds.

During the second half of the game, Valerie hands out her Homecoming Queen flyers. Honestly, I think she has a better chance of winning than Susan. Susan is not very popular and she isn't trying hard at all.

Now there are fourteen seconds left in the game, and the Titans are winning, seventeen to fourteen. We have the ball. Valerie starts our chant again, and the entire crowd joins in.

After he gets the ball, Ricky shuffles back and forth for a second, looking for a receiver. The only one open is Romeo and he's near the end zone. It's a long pass, but

Ricky throws it all the way down the field. Romeo just has to catch it.

And he does! We win the game with zero seconds left on the clock.

The Hi-Steppers and about half the fans clear the stands and spill out onto the field. I'm so proud of Ricky that I literally jump into his arms and give him a gigantic hug.

"Whoa!" he says.

"Good game, Ricky!"

I think we hold our embrace for just a second too long, because Ricky steps away from me like he's uncomfortable or something. It's all good, though. I just got a little carried away in the post-game excitement.

I'm serious.

Whatever. I know what you're thinking and you're so the opposite of right.

Hope joins Ricky and me on the field. "You did awesome, Ricky!"

"The entire team did a good job," he says.

To get to FunNStuff, everyone grabs a ride with someone driving, because it's about twenty minutes away from the school. Of course, we've got our normal car group—Ricky, Kevin, Hope, and me. And . . . ugh . . . Candy.

Ricky's changed out of his uniform, and whatever he splashed on in the locker room smells mighty nice. What? I'm just saying. Can I not enjoy pleasant scents?

Candy says, "Ricky, what did you do, spray on the whole bottle?"

"You know, people would like you more if you were a little sweeter," Ricky replies.

"But then they wouldn't really like me, right? They'd like some fake person that is not me. I'm just gonna do me. Regardless."

Pfft . . . Whatever! I've never seen more fakeness than when Candy is around Valerie. She gets the boo-I-don't-believe-you side eye.

When we get to FunNStuff, there is a small crowd at the front door. I guess just about everyone came over from the game, because I see mostly Longfellow Spartans in the mix.

As we make it to the front of the line, Ricky taps me on the shoulder. "That's what's holding us up." He points toward the door where Romeo and Valerie stand, handing out flyers.

"She really wants this Homecoming queen thing *bad,* doesn't she?" I ask.

"Pretty much," Ricky whispers.

Valerie smiles at us and hands Ricky a flyer. "Are you gonna vote for me, Rick?" she asks.

"Uh, I guess," he replies. Clearly, she caught him off guard.

"Will you wear a button too?" Valerie asks, her voice sounding like a purr.

Ricky swallows. "S-sure. I guess so."

Valerie steps closer to Ricky. "You guess? I want you to be sure."

Ricky shudders when Valerie takes one of her buttons and pins it on his jacket. I'm not sure if the shudder is from fear of being stuck or the fact that Valerie is basically nose to nose with Ricky *and* she's wearing that strawberry lip gloss.

Hope fumes. I think I can literally see the steam coming from the top of her head.

"I thought you said she was done," Hope hisses in my ear.

"Well, she said she was done," I reply in my defense.

"I sure can't tell."

Finally, Ricky pulls himself away from Valerie and we go inside. The only lighting inside is coming from the ton of arcade games that are all over the huge loft-like building. Hope sees some of her rally girl friends and waves at them.

"Ricky, Gia, I'm gonna go say hello to my rally sisters. I'll be right back, okay?" Hope's smile is on overdrive, and even though she said my name in that sentence, she is clearly talking to Ricky alone.

Kevin laughs as Hope jogs away. "Ricky, can you please just be her boyfriend? This is getting kind of old."

"True that!" Candy exclaims. "You are spitting truth, Kev."

Kevin's eyes light up. "I am! Awesome!"

Candy looks Kevin up and down and giggles. "You are just extra excited, aren't you? My friends are here too, so I'm ready to bounce. Where are we gonna meet when it's time to go?"

"Meet me at the door at eleven fifteen," Ricky says. "That ought to give us enough time to get home by curfew."

"Cool!"

Gwen showed mercy on us tonight and extended curfew to midnight.

Candy joins Valerie and the rest of the Hi-Steppers. Kevin has the audacity to look disappointed. Boo, Kevin!

"So y'all wanna play laser tag?" I ask.

Ricky grins. "I didn't think you'd want to be punished tonight."

"Punished? Boy, I will crush you. Let's do this!"

This is the Ricky I know and love. Er . . . strongly like. I like when he maintains his homeboy status, and I also love beating him at games. He needs to simmer down with all his girlfriend and Homecoming drama.

But at this point, it is what it is. I just hope we spend the rest of the school year having more fun and less foolishness!

★ 21 ★

"Last night was fun, huh?" Candy asks.

She's got her morning breath all up in my personal space and I'm completely unappreciative. I put my pillow over my head.

Candy is talking about the rally girls' party. It *was* fun. Hope and I totally creamed Ricky and Kevin in laser tag.

"So we're going to Valerie's party tonight, right?" Candy clearly doesn't care that my eyes haven't yet opened.

Candy taps the bottom of my foot. "Wake up, Gia! We've got to go to the mall and get fly outfits for Valerie's hayride. What do you wear to a hayride, anyway?"

This makes me remove my pillow. "Jeans, jean jacket, boots. But I'm not going to the mall with you, Candy. Not today, not ever."

"Whatever, Gia! You get on my nerves. I do have money, by the way."

I get on her nerves? I'm going to have to say ditto to

that emotion. Besides, I'm not the one who plans my own personal cash-free shopping sprees.

"Even if you do have money, I'm not going. I've got to go to the library with Ricky and Kevin to finish our English paper. Sorry."

"I'll just call my friends then. It's cool."

Suddenly, our bedroom door swings open. "Rise and shine, girls! We're going out for breakfast," Gwen announces.

"Where are we going to eat? Is it near the library, because I have to meet Kevin and Ricky there at noon."

"We're going to IHOP, Gia. You'll get to the library in plenty of time." Gwen sounds a bit irritated, like I'm trying to rain on her parade or something.

I ask, "Candy, when are you meeting with your friends at the mall?"

Gwen narrows her eyes suspiciously. "I can take you shopping. What do you need?"

Candy smiles. "We were going to do more hanging than shopping. If it's okay with you, I'd rather have my dad drop me off this afternoon."

"Fine with me," Gwen says, "but both of you be ready in thirty minutes. I want some pancakes."

When Gwen closes the door, Candy whispers, "I don't want to go to breakfast with Gwen."

I laugh out loud. "It could be worse. She could be trying to make the pancakes herself."

Candy is straight killing me. Wasn't she just calling my mother Mama Gwen a couple of weeks ago? Now that Gwen is on the trail, Candy doesn't want anything to do with her. Too bad for Candy, Gwen doesn't give up that easily, and once she decides to catch you in some dirt, you're pretty much caught.

We're sitting in one of IHOP's booths and I'm reading through the menu like I don't already know what I want. I've been getting the same thing ever since Ricky and I discovered our favorite—big, fluffy pancakes topped with hot apples and whipped cream. Yummy!

Gwen orders blueberry pancakes and Candy selects an omelet, probably due to Valerie's ban on carbohydrates. Valerie can fall back with that mess. Nobody is gonna stop me from eating bread products, especially pancakes!

While we're waiting on our food, I see Gwen get that *mother-daughter talk* face. I'm sooo not interested in that this early in the morning!

"So where are you girls going this evening? Anywhere fun?" Gwen asks.

I say, "Mom, we're going to the hayride, remember?"

"That's right! Some things never go out of style, I guess. We used to have hayrides when I was in school. They were so much fun, especially for us cheerleaders."

"You were a cheerleader, Mama Gwen?" Candy asks. Hush my mouth. She actually sounds interested.

"Yes, honey! I was the captain of the football and basketball cheerleaders until I got pregnant with Gia my senior year. Then I had to drop everything."

Candy looks sad, as if the story touched her. "That's horrible you had to quit the squad! I bet you cried your eyes out."

"I was definitely sad about everything I missed out on during my senior year," Gwen says with a reflective look on her face. "I learned a good life lesson in it though."

Since I've heard this already, I allow Candy to ask the questions. "What did you learn, Mama Gwen?"

"I learned that for every action, there's a reaction, and for every decision there is a consequence."

I yawn and look around for the food. I need to teach Candy the rules about Gwen's lectures. Endure with as little input as possible, and respond with nods and smiles only. It makes it easer for everyone.

"Candy, I know I'm not your mother, but you can come to me anytime you feel like you're in over your head or in trouble. Just like you go to your mom and dad."

Gwen is offering the peace treaty. I knew this was coming, but I also knew she wasn't going to let Candy feel like she got over by snitching to her father.

"Thanks. I'll keep that in mind." Candy doesn't look like she really means that, but Gwen still has a hopeful expression on her face.

If I wasn't a very strong and fabulous young lady, I might be a little irritated about *my* mother working overtime to win Candy over. And since I *am* fab all day and all night, I am not going to mention to anyone the lack of work LeRon has done in trying to win *me* over.

"What is the matter with you, Gia? You seem stressed," Kevin says.

I draw a doodle flower in the corner of my notebook page. "Nothing. Let's just finish this story."

Ricky asks, "So are Steve and Helena getting together or what?"

"I don't care," I reply. "Why should *they* get a happy ending?"

Kevin and Ricky stare at me. Okay, yeah, I know I'm acting snippy. Maybe, in spite of my fabulosity, I *am* more than a little irritated about this whole Candy situation.

"What is wrong with you?" Ricky asks. "And don't say nothing. Because it's not nothing. It is definitely something, and your something is keeping us from finishing this story! And I'm trying to get an A!"

And I'm the one who's stressed? Ya think?

"Okay, I'll tell you, but only if you stop tripping. Good grief, Ricky!"

Ricky takes a deep breath and then exhales. "All right. I'm good. Now spill it!"

"It's really about Candy," I start.

Kevin's eyes light up. "What about Candy?"

"Eww, Kevin. Simmer down. This is serious."

"Sorry, Gia."

"Like I was saying, it's about Candy. Everyone in our house is so concerned with making her happy and comfortable. My mom and her dad."

"So what's wrong with that?" Ricky asks.

"Well, nothing except that LeRon acts like I'm some loose girl who's gonna run off with every boy I see."

"You're looking at two boys right now," Kevin says.

"Exactly! But if you ask LeRon, I'm going to corrupt his precious little baby girl."

"So what are you gonna do about it?" Ricky asks.

I slam my pencil down on the table. "What *can* I do? How can I prove him wrong?"

Kevin frowns seriously. "Well, I guess all you can do is not prove him right."

★ **22** ★

By Kevin's choice, Steve and Helena live happily ever after and go on to have a huge wedding at their church. Yes, that ending totally belongs to Kevin. I wanted Steve and Helena to run off to an island and get married on the beach. But Kevin just *had* to have a church scene in the story. I should've known there would be no way to work with Kevin on a school project and not include a church scene.

I'm almost home from the library, but I'm taking my time walking down the street. Ricky had offered to give me a ride, but I refused. I actually wanted to walk home. It's not often that I get to hear my own thoughts anymore. Having alone time is not really all that realistic in the Ferguson household.

As I turn down our street, I think about what Kevin said. There's no way I'm gonna prove that LeRon is right about his bad impression of me. But I wonder how long it will take for *him* to believe it.

Okay, so why is there a police car in our driveway?

I say a quick prayer as I run the rest of the way and through the door. *Lord, please let my mom be okay.*

My prayer is immediately answered because Gwen is definitely okay. In fact she looks furious, and so does LeRon. Candy is sitting on the couch in tears, as the police officer talks to both of our parents.

"We had pictures of Candy and her friends hanging in the security office at the mall," the officer explains. "They were on our watch list, after reviewing several store surveillance video tapes."

LeRon says, "There's got to be some mistake. My daughter doesn't *have* to steal! She gets everything that she wants!"

I watch in shock as the police officer hands LeRon photos to look at. Gwen reaches for the photographs too, but LeRon tries to snatch them away. My mother is quicker, though, and she gets her hands on one of the pictures.

Gwen shakes her head. "This is definitely Candy. Girl, what do you have to say for yourself?"

"I don't have to say anything to you!" Candy yells through her sobs. "I want my mother!"

I close the front door and everyone turns to look at me. Through all of the excitement, I guess they didn't see me come in.

Gwen says, "Gia, go to your room, honey. You can get ready for the hayride."

"She's not going to that hayride!" exclaims LeRon.

"She's the reason for all of this anyway. I knew she would be a bad influence on Candy."

"What!" I scream at the top of my lungs.

Gwen puts one hand up to stop me from completely letting loose. "Don't worry, Gia. I got this."

Then she turns to LeRon and says, "You are not going to punish Gia for Candy's mistakes. I don't see Gia in any of those pictures."

LeRon ignores Gwen and asks the police officer, "Is *she* on your watch list?" He points at me when he asks this.

The officer narrows his eyes and looks closely at me. "No sir, she's not."

LeRon drops his head and gives Candy the most disgusted side-eye I've ever seen.

Gwen says, "Thank you, officer. Gia, go ahead to your room. Ricky will probably be here to pick you up in a couple of hours."

"Thanks, Mom."

I take one last glance at Candy before I go to the bedroom. She looks so pitiful that I actually feel bad for her. But she can't say that she wasn't sufficiently warned.

Since I don't really have anything else to do, I search through my clothes for a hayride-appropriate ensemble. Although I rarely wear skirts, I decide on a knee-length jean skirt and matching jacket. I match it up with my cream colored Tweety tee and knee-high brown pleather boots. Fierce and fab all at the same time!

As I'm digging through my jewelry box looking for my gold hoop earrings, Candy plods quietly into the room.

She says absolutely nothing as she climbs the bunk-bed ladder and throws herself across her bed.

"How bad did they ground you?" I ask.

"They haven't decided on my punishment yet. But my dad won't let your mother come up with anything too crazy."

I chuckle to myself because Candy is a trip. I don't see how she can still think she's on top of the world, when her world is over!

"My mom is usually pretty fair about punishment. I think it's your father that you have to worry about."

I mean this too. Since my mother married LeRon all he's done is come up with ways to punish me for nothing. And I'm not even going to talk about how he tried to punish me for Candy's shoplifting! I'm still too angry to go there.

As soon as we hear the police car pull out of the driveway, our bedroom door swings open. LeRon and Gwen are together and they both look furious enough to end someone's life. I'm so glad that someone isn't me.

"Candy, empty your drawers," LeRon says.

"Why?" she asks, as if she's in a position to ask questions. Has she *ever* been punished?

"Having designer clothes seems very important to you. More important than how we feel or how God feels," Gwen says.

"So we're going to take them away," LeRon adds. The finality in his tone scares me. I'm literally afraid of what they're gonna do.

"Daddy, no!" Candy cries out in desperation.

LeRon is not moved at all. "Candy, get down from

that bunk bed and empty your drawers and your side of the closet."

"Make sure you get all of that grown-woman underwear out of there too," Gwen adds.

I see that Gwen has an extra problem with Candy's lacy Victoria's Secret underwear. I don't see how she wears that stuff anyway. It looks like a pile of strings with ribbons tied to the ends. It totally does not look comfortable.

I sit down at my desk to watch, because the only place Candy has to pile her things is on my bed. She has more stuff than I even knew about. She's got about twenty pairs of Seven and Lucky Brand jeans, an assortment of Baby Phat, DKNY, and House of Deréon outfits, and designer T-shirts galore.

Then she starts on the shoes. Pair after pair of Nike tennis shoes, designer boots, and designer heels are tossed into the middle of the floor.

"Don't forget those purses," LeRon says.

"I didn't take some of this stuff," Candy wails. "You and my *real mother* gave me some of this for my birthdays and Christmas."

Gwen chuckles. "Guess what, sweetie. Your real mother is just as disgusted with you as we are, so don't think you're going to get any sympathy from her."

When Candy finally empties out everything, she has the audacity to ask, "What are you going to do with my stuff?"

LeRon replies, "I think all of this high-priced stuff will be perfect donations for the battered women's shelter run by the church, don't you, Gwen?"

"You are absolutely correct," Gwen gushes.

"So what am I gonna wear?" Candy asks.

Gwen smiles and leaves the room. Candy is wearing a defiant expression on her face, like she doesn't have any intention of following any punishment that's handed down. I'm just in awe and somewhat relieved that it's not happening to me.

Gwen reappears with a ridiculous-looking jogging suit that went out of style before I was born, and some Dollar Store tennis shoes. The jogging suit is a crazy, bright shade of green and the shoes are blue with purple stripes.

"What is that?" Candy asks.

Gwen laughs. "Oh, it's your new favorite outfit!"

Candy bursts into tears. I can truly feel her pain because never in a thousand years did I think they'd come up with something like this. Cruel and unusual punishment comes to mind.

LeRon says, "Gwen and I will save five tops and five bottoms from this pile of clothing, things that I'm sure I paid money for."

"But for an entire week, you're going to wear this outfit."

Gwen tosses the items to Candy, but she lets them fall to the floor. She refuses to touch the clown-like clothes as tears stream down her face. It seems like LeRon and Gwen have attended some school of medieval punishment. They definitely had to put their heads together to come up with this. I don't know if Gwen is capable of this much evil on her own.

LeRon explains, "Each week you'll earn back one outfit, until you've earned all five of the saved outfits."

"Then what?" Candy asks.

"Then, you'll wear those clothes and only those until spring break."

Candy throws her head back and wails. "Daddy, you're going to ruin my life! Pleeease don't do this to me!"

"It's called a consequence, Candy. It's something, I'm afraid, that you haven't experienced enough," LeRon says sadly.

Candy's eyes open wide. "But what about the Hi-Steppers? I'll be cut from the squad if I only have five outfits."

I lift my eyebrows with interest. Of course, Valerie will treat Candy like a pariah and, of course, that means Jewel and Kelani will follow. But I am co-captain. I should be able to keep her from getting kicked off the squad.

I clear my throat and say nervously, "I think that I can talk to Mrs. Vaughn. She'll understand that it's a punishment."

Candy narrows her eyes angrily at me, as if I'm not helping her cause. Well, I know she doesn't think that Gwen or LeRon are gonna have mercy on her over the Hi-Steppers. That's sooo not about to happen.

LeRon gathers Candy's belongings in armfuls and takes them out of the room slowly. Gwen zooms in on one of the handbags sitting on the floor. She walks over and picks up the oversized Louis Vuitton bag.

"Candy, is this real?" she asks.

Candy nods and another tear escapes down her cheek.

Gwen cracks a half-smile. "Well, I will say one thing, you have got great taste."

"A lot of good that's gonna do me," Candy says with a pout. She kicks out at her punishment clothes as if they are garbage.

LeRon finishes gathering Candy's clothes and stands in the center of the room. "In addition to your clothing punishment, you are not allowed to go anywhere but to school, Hi-Steppers rehearsal, church, and home. No television, no cell phone, no internet, and no texting. Nothing for a month."

"What about the football games?" Candy asks frantically. "I'm on the Hi-Steppers A squad."

Gwen turns to me. "Do you think you can talk to Mrs. Vaughn about this? Can someone fill in for Candy until her punishment is over?"

"Probably so. I'll ask her."

"Thanks."

I don't mention that the football season will be over before Candy's punishment is. That just kinda of feels like kicking someone when they're down. Candy won't get to wear those little white boots again until next school year.

Candy glares at me again, as if I'm her mortal enemy. I don't want her to feel this way, but part of me feels like she's getting what she deserves. And LeRon has this really melancholy expression on his face like he didn't see this one coming.

Well, maybe if he hadn't been so worried about what I was doing . . .

Wait a minute. I'm still not even going to go there, because this thing is all bad for everybody involved, including me. Candy has just now invited an extra level of surveillance down on both of us. Not that I'm planning anything sneaky, but if I was, there'd be no way I'd be able to pull it off. It's gonna be like Alcatraz up in this piece.

As soon as Gwen and LeRon leave the room and close the door, Candy crumples to the floor in a little ball. She sobs uncontrollably, as if she's the only one in the room. I can feel the sadness rolling from her body in waves, like it's trying to reach out and grab me.

For reasons I can't explain, I feel my feet taking themselves over to Candy. I'm so not trying to play the comforting big sister right now, but I can't help myself. I put both my arms around Candy and squeeze her tightly.

"Don't worry, Candy. It's only clothes."

Candy doesn't reply, but her sobs quiet a little. I guess she's gonna need all the support she can get from me over the next few weeks. Because if she thinks LeRon and Gwen are cruel, wait until she gets a load of Valerie.

Umm . . . yeah . . . Candy is in for it.

★ 23 ★

I'm waiting outside when Ricky gets to my house. I don't want my friends to come in and see the aftermath of Candy's activities. Gwen is still furious and LeRon is in a really weird mood. He looks like he's on the verge of tears, but he's not letting them fall.

It's so cold tonight that I changed my mind about the jean skirt, and instead put on jeans that match my jacket. I'm sure most other girls will have on cute jean and corduroy skirts, but a sista like me is not trying to get frostbite to make a fashion statement. On top of my whole ensemble is a silver down jacket with a nice furry hood.

As I walk up to the car, I see that Ricky has already picked up Kevin and Hope. I smirk to myself when I notice that Hope has figured a way to get in the front seat with Ricky. It's like she kicked her chase into high gear once Valerie stepped out of the way.

I've got to give it to my cousin. She is definitely persistent.

"Where's Candy?" Kevin asks as I blow warm air into my hands, trying to thaw them.

"Umm . . . she's not coming." This is the only answer I can come up with, without putting all her business out there.

"Why? Is she sick?" Hope asks.

"No."

Ricky narrows his eyes and peers at me through the rearview mirror. "Spill it, Gia. I know you're hiding something."

That's the trouble with best friends. There is no way I can hide any kind of juicy scoop from Ricky.

"She's on punishment," I say.

Hope's eyes get big as she asks, "Did she get caught boosting?"

I nod slowly. It doesn't count as me blabbing if they figure it out, right?

"Oh, Lord. Gia, have you been praying for her?" Kevin asks.

This boy is a trip! "Have *you* been praying for her?"

"Yes, of course. I was praying that she'd see the error of her ways and stop."

"Well, then your prayers are partially answered," I say. "I don't know if she believes she was wrong, but I guarantee you that she's gonna stop. Absolutely and without a doubt."

"Did Auntie Gwen go crazy on her?" Hope asks.

Hope knows how Gwen gets down. She's been a witness to some of Gwen's worst scenes. Like the time when Hope and I were six and we thought Gwen's sewing room would look better with smiley faces spray-painted on the wall. Um, yeah . . . it was all bad.

"Gwen was pretty calm, but LeRon was tripping," I reply.

Ricky asks, "What did he do?"

"First of all, he tried to blame me for Candy's issues."

"No, he didn't!" Hope says with surprise in her tone.

"He sooo did! He even tried to stop me from coming tonight."

Ricky says, "That's not cool. What did Gwen say about that?"

"Well, obviously she didn't let him get out on me like that. I'm here, aren't I?"

Kevin asks, "So what did they do to Candy? She's still in the land of the living, right?"

Land of the living? Hahahahaha! Kevin has been making so much progress, but at one sign of trouble he drops all freshness and goes back to old-school church language. He sounds like his grandmother getting ready to testify on Sunday. She always says, *Lord, I thank you for keeping me in the land of the living.* Boo, Kevin!!!!

"Miss Candy is cool," I say. "Her wardrobe is going to be rather . . . limited . . . over the next few weeks or so, but she's cool."

"What do you mean by that?" Hope asks.

"I think I'll just let you see her on Monday and judge for yourself."

"That bad, huh?" Ricky asks.

"Even worse . . ."

*　　*　　*

So, I'm trying to figure out this whole hayride concept. A lot of young people get together and ride around an open field in a big wooden wagon pulled by a tractor. Inside the wooden wagon is a bunch of dry, itchy hay. Let's not forget how cold it is out here; it's about forty degrees at the most, but at least it's dry.

Tell me why I'm here again?

Oh yeah, because all of the freshest, flyest, and most popular kids have decided that this is the fun thing to do. Remind me to not go along with this foolishness next year.

Hope whispers in my ear, "I'm going to sit next to Ricky in the wagon."

Of course she's going to sit next to Ricky in the wagon. Or at least she'll try. But I want to know why I have to be included in every single decision Hope makes in reference to Ricky. Her un-reciprocated (okay . . . not sure if that's a word) affection irritates me beyond reason.

I snap. "Listen, Hope. If you're going to make a play for Ricky just do it. Don't tell me about it."

"But why wouldn't I tell you? You're my cousin and Ricky's best friend!"

"You know I hate drama," I say with a sigh. "And you, Ricky, and Valerie have given me more than my fair share."

"I didn't know you felt that way," Hope says.

"Now you do."

"I wonder," Hope continues, "if it's more than your aversion to drama that makes you so annoyed with this love triangle."

Love triangle? This girl is beyond delusional. Don't you need three people to form a triangle? The only ones catching feelings are her and Valerie. They've got a love line segment (no . . . I absolutely will not explain that. Simple geometry, people. Elevate your mind).

"What are you trying to say?" I ask, feeling even *more* annoyed.

"I think maybe you're blocking because you are feeling Ricky more than you admit."

"Whatever, Hope. I'm not even going to entertain that. I am *not* blocking either, by the way. I'm just pointing out the obvious."

Hope lifts an eyebrow at me and says, "I'm not blind, Gia. You and Ricky are perfect for each other. You both like to make up corny dance steps, and y'all both use slang that no one else is using. I'm really surprised that you haven't already tried to holla at him."

Seriously? Is she trying to analyze me? She best not quit her day job, on the real. Ricky and I do have a lot in common. Hello! That's why we're best friends!

"Listen, just don't involve me in your romance with Ricky and we'll be just fine."

"Okay."

"Thank you! Was that so hard?"

Valerie struts up to us looking like she's about to board a plane to Aspen. Her light brown suede jacket and skirt is the business! She's wearing thick cream-colored tights and matching suede boots. Her makeup even matches her clothing. I know she's cold because her cheeks are a bright red, rosy color, but it only seems to add to her fresh factor!

Dang her!

"Are you having fun, chica?" This question is directed to me, because Valerie prefers to pretend that Hope does not exist.

"We are having a great time!" Hope answers for both of us.

Valerie sneers at Hope and says, "We're about to serve dinner soon in the barn. And then we'll go on the hayride. After that, we're gonna square dance."

Square dance? Okay, somebody is tripping. I don't square dance. I don't do anything square.

Ricky and Kevin jog over to us. "Did someone say dinner?" Kevin asks.

"Yes." Valerie grins at Ricky while answering Kevin's question.

I grab Valerie's arm to hold her in place and say to Ricky, "Hey, y'all, save me a seat at the dinner table. I need to talk to Valerie a second."

Ricky looks suspicious but says, "Okay, Gi-Gi. See you inside."

When I've pulled Valerie a safe distance away from everyone I ask, "Are you done with Ricky or not? It sure doesn't seem like it."

"I'm done pursuing him. That's not how I get down. I don't chase boys . . . they chase me. But if Ricky ever comes to his senses, then I would definitely be open for a reunion."

I nod, satisfied with her surprisingly honest answer. "Okay, cool."

Valerie lets out a flurry of giggles. I frown because I have no idea what is so funny.

She says, "You just seem super concerned, that's all. I

wish that you and Ricky would stop playing games and just hook up already."

Okay, two times in one night is too much. I stalk away from Valerie without answering her accusation. Of course, I would be open to taking my friendship with Ricky to the boyfriend level. But the *hook up* level? Um . . . big, fat *no, ma 'am!*

Plus, all of their theories about Ricky and me would hinge on Ricky actually having romantic feelings about me. And I haven't seen evidence of this at all. My only not-so-secret admirer, Kevin, even seems to be slipping away into the clutches of Candy.

So, I'm pretty much romance free.

I make my way into the huge barn where they're serving dinner. It smells like barbeque, which makes my stomach growl. I haven't had any good barbeque in a long time. I've had the disgusting, burnt-to-a-crisp substitute that Gwen *calls* barbeque, but not the real thing.

Ricky waves me over to their table. I see a place saved for me, but I also see that Hope has strategically gotten herself a seat next to Ricky. I guess she plans to be right up under him all evening.

Poor Ricky.

I take my seat at the table and say, "It smells good in here. I'm starving."

"Yeah, the menu says that they have ribs and chicken, corn on the cob, and potato salad," Kevin says.

I wonder how much Valerie's mother spent on this shindig. I know that they've got dough and all, but dang! This had to cost like sweet-sixteen-party kind of money.

All to win a Homecoming-queen crown? Wow on top of wow.

As if to answer my question Hope says, "Valerie's uncle owns this place. I heard he threw this party as a gift to her."

Valerie's mother stands in front of about three hundred kids from Longfellow High with a microphone. "Hola, everyone! Tonight we're having this party in honor of my Valerie, my hija." She rolls her *r* as she says *Valerie,* making it sound more like *Valerrrie.*

"Everybody can line up for the dinner, and there is plenty of food for everyone!" Valerie's mom announces, and places the microphone back in its cradle.

We line up with the rest of the crowd. As we wait to get our food, Valerie walks up and down the line with Romeo, giving people buttons and urging them to vote for her. Romeo is only a junior and not even running for Homecoming court, so I don't see what's in it for him. It seems like he's content to be Valerie's date for the evening.

Hope leans in and whispers, "I wonder what secret Valerie has on Romeo. I heard she knows something about him that can get him thrown off the football team."

"I heard the same thing," I reply.

Even though it was last school year, I remember like it was yesterday, the conversation that I overheard between Valerie, Kelani, and Jewel. They were talking about how badly Romeo was playing me, and Valerie admitted to forcing Romeo to date me to keep me out of her way while she schemed on Ricky. She claimed to have a huge secret on him that pretty much made him her slave.

I wonder what could be that awful.

The giggle clones, Jewel and Kelani, walk up to us. Surprisingly, they look pretty cute with their matching corduroy hookups and Timberland boots. They're each wearing two long, braided ponytails with little brown bows on the ends.

"So where's your sister?" Kelani asks.

"Who, Candy?"

Jewel laughs. "How many other sisters do you have?"

Yes, I knew she was talking about Candy, but sometimes it takes a moment to register that she's actually my sister. I've been an only child for so long that sometimes it feels crazy to say I have a sister.

"Candy's at home," I reply. "She couldn't make it tonight."

Kelani scrunches her nose. "What do you mean, she couldn't make it? This is a Hi-Stepper party. There's no excuse for her not making it."

I decide to let Candy explain her situation to Jewel and Kelani, because once they find out what has happened, they will tell the entire school. That would be messed up if Candy walked in the school on Monday with everyone already knowing about her punishment.

"Why don't y'all ask her on Monday morning?"

Jewel narrows her eyes and stares me down like she thinks I'm hiding something. "I'm gonna send her a text right now."

I don't bother to tell her that Candy doesn't have her phone and probably won't have it back anytime soon.

On our way back to the table Ricky holds my arm and lets Hope and Kevin walk way ahead of us. Then he answers my unasked question by whispering in my ear, "Please sit next to me on the hayride."

What part of the game is this? I promise that I don't want to be in the middle of this mess, and every time I'm almost out, they keep pulling me back in!

I stop in my tracks and Ricky turns around when he realizes I'm no longer next to him. "What's wrong?" he asks as he walks back to me.

"Ricky, you're gonna have to tell Hope that you don't like her. She'll kill me if I sit next to you. You can't keep using me to block for you."

Ricky sighs. "You're right. I'm gonna tell her tonight."

As we sit down at the table, Hope gives me a strange look. "What took y'all so long?"

Ricky clears his throat. "I had to ask Gia something."

"Something like what?" Hope asks, her eyebrows lifted way up and also questioning.

"Has anyone ever told you how nosy you are?" I ask.

"No," Ricky says. "I want to tell her."

Now Hope looks worried. "You want to tell me what?"

"I asked Gia to sit next to me on the hayride."

"You did?" Hope asks with panic in her tone.

"Yes. I asked her that, because I didn't want to have to tell you no."

"I don't understand," Hope says with a quiver in her voice.

"Hope, you know that I love you as my sister in Christ, but I don't want you to be my girlfriend."

Hope takes a deep breath and says, "Okay . . ."

"It's not that you're not pretty, because you are," Ricky rambles, "but I'm not ready for a girlfriend right now, and it would make it so much easier if you would stop trying. Not that I don't appreciate it, because I'm flattered. But please stop . . . okay?"

My eyes and Kevin's eyes dart from Ricky's face to Hope's face. I have a countdown going on in my mind to when Hope's tears are gonna start. I guess Ricky has nothing left to say because he plugs his mouth with a huge forkful of potato salad.

"Thank you for telling me, Ricky," Hope says sadly. "Do you all mind if I sit with the rally girls right now? It's just a little embarrassing to stay here for now."

"We understand," I say, releasing Hope to go and nurse her wounds.

Kevin and I both stare at Ricky. "What?" he asks. "Isn't this what you wanted me to do?"

"Yes, I guess so, I just didn't think she'd take it that hard," I reply. "She looked like she was about to start crying."

"I know. But I'll still be nice to her," Ricky says.

Kevin responds, "I'd be careful on the being nice bit. Just let her get over it, and don't say anything to her. That will make it easier for her."

"Wow, Kev. That was freakishly insightful. I didn't know you knew anything about girls."

Kevin chuckles. "A lot of good it does me."

After dinner, we're handed little tickets for the hayride. Because there are so many kids here, it's gonna take a minute to get through everyone. Valerie and Romeo are riding on each trip because Valerie is still, of course, campaigning for Homecoming queen.

While we're waiting for our turn, we take cups of

warm apple cider and chill in front of the huge fire pit. Someone has broken out a bag of marshmallows too. As much as I hate to admit it, this is probably the most fun party I've been to all year.

Fellow football player, James, asks Ricky, "Dude, why aren't you campaigning? Aren't you running for Homecoming prince?"

"Someone submitted my name, but I can't exactly say that I'm running," Ricky replies.

"Dude, you better represent for the Spartans!" James exclaims.

Kevin and I giggle. We know how much the subject of Homecoming court annoys Ricky.

"I'm voting for Ricky!" Kelani says. "I think he'd be cute with that little crown and robe on."

Ricky blushes. "Um . . . thanks, I think. But I think Romeo wants it more than I do. You should vote for him."

Ricky looks all kinds of relieved when our ticket numbers are finally called for the hayride. He doesn't do so well under pressure. It makes me wonder how he's such a good football player.

I take a seat between Kevin and Ricky. For warmth mostly, and not because of Ricky's previous request. Fortunately, Hope is not on this ride. I'd hate for her to hurt anymore this evening. She's already been through enough.

Valerie sits directly opposite us and Romeo is at her side. Romeo's arm is around Valerie and she snuggles up close to him while gazing at Ricky. Ricky looks away under her intense stare.

As we ride around in the cold with our warm breath

blowing vapors in the wind, I think about how far Ricky and I have come. We are definitely a part of the popular crowd, even if we're on the fringes. Last year, before I became a Hi-Stepper, and when Ricky was a second-string quarterback, we weren't getting invited to anything. But now, our social calendar is off the charts.

It's pretty unbelievable.

★ 24 ★

"I'm not going to church! You can't make me!"
It is way too early in the morning for this foolishness. I got in late from the hayride, and I'd like to get another fifteen minutes of sleep, but I can see that's not going to happen! Ugh!

Candy is standing about five inches from my bed and LeRon is outside the closed bedroom door.

"Why do you think you're not going to church, Candy? We always go every Sunday, as a family."

Candy replies, "I don't think God cares about me. If He did, He wouldn't let you and your wife torture me."

"Stop being melodramatic, Candy, and get dressed."

"You're going to have to flog me, like they did the Apostle Paul."

LeRon ignores Candy. "Gia. It's time to get up. We're going to be late for Sunday school. Candy, get your clothes on."

"Yea, though I walk through the valley of the shadow of death . . . I fear no evil!" Candy wails.

I have to stifle my giggles, because this is some funny stuff!

"Candy, I'm not playing around with you." LeRon sounds irritated. "Get dressed!"

Candy takes a long pause and then replies, "The Lord is my shepherd, I shall not want!"

"Candy, I'm counting to five, and if you're not in the bathroom, you're going to be praying for real." LeRon's voice sounds like a booming roar. It's finally enough to get some action out of Candy.

"Girl, do you like playing with fire?" I ask as Candy finally grabs her clothes.

"He won't do anything he says. I guarantee that I'll have a pile of new outfits by the end of the week. I've already got back some of my skirts and dresses. This is just step one in my process."

"That's just because my mother didn't want you to wear that clown suit to church. But I wouldn't push it."

I'm glad she's so confident and sure of herself. I don't tell her that I think her daddy might be a little bit stronger with Gwen backing him up. I figure they can show her better than I can tell her.

There's another knock on our door. "Girls, I'm making eggs. Do y'all want scrambled or fried?" Gwen asks.

Mmm-kay, the answer is neither. Besides, there are only two kinds of eggs with Gwen—burnt and half-raw. I vote no.

"I'll take scrambled, Mama Gwen!" Candy replies in a sing-song voice.

"Okay, Candy. Coming right up. What about you, Gia?"

"I'll just have a piece of toast." She can't mess that up, right?

"All right then."

I roll my eyes at Candy. "Please tell me that buttering Gwen up isn't step two in your process."

Candy just smiles. "Watch and learn. Watch and learn."

Since this Sunday isn't a youth choir Sunday, we are forced to listen to the mass choir. I'm not going to say that they're bad, but the adult choir director, Sister Pennington, is deaf in one ear. Plus, she's one of those people who thinks that any- and everybody who wants to sing should be in the choir. She doesn't turn anyone away. Not even Sister Butler, who sounds like she has a chainsaw in her throat.

I can barely keep my eyes open during their especially unrousing rendition of "We Lift Our Hands in the Sanctuary." Man, Kurt Carr would probably ban our church from ever singing his lively song again if he heard our choir mangle it.

Ricky, who is ushering this week, sits down next to me on the back pew. He looks exhausted.

"Hey, Gia. Did you get enough sleep last night?"

"No way. If Pastor preaches long today, I guarantee I'm falling asleep."

Ricky laughs. "You better not. You know that Gwen will come back here and pinch you like you're four years old."

"I know it, but I'm afraid I won't be able to help myself."

Hope slips into the sanctuary, also looking beat. She gives me and Ricky some very conspicuous side eye. I mean, she doesn't even try to hide it.

"Do you think she's still mad at me?" Ricky asks.

"I think she's gonna be mad at you for a minute. Just give her some time, okay?"

Kevin's grandmother, Mother Witherspoon, is shooting Ricky some head-usher evil eye. A whole family of visitors walked in and took a seat without a program or a fan. In Mother Witherspoon's book that is nothing short of blasphemy. I won't be surprised if she makes Ricky go down to the altar and repent.

Pastor Stokes finally takes the podium, and I groan out loud when I see he's wearing a comfortable suit. That means he's settling in for a nice hour-long sermon. Why today of all days? When all I want to do is go back home and crash.

He's preaching about loving our enemies. I glance over at Elder LeRon sitting in the pulpit along with my uncle. It feels like LeRon is almost an enemy, even though I know he loves my mother.

How could he blame Candy's problems on me? And even after he knew I wasn't involved, how could he not apologize? That is so the opposite of right.

After a quite merciful thirty-five minutes, Pastor Stokes is done. You don't think thirty-five minutes is merciful? Well, he's been known to go for an hour and a half when he wears his comfortable suit, so I consider myself blessed today!

I go over to Mother Cranford after service. I know she's not speaking to me, because I've truly been neglecting her on the weekends. I never expected my life to get so busy and complicated.

"Well, lookee here. It's my long-lost employee," Mother Cranford says as I place a light kiss on her cheek.

"Mother, you know it's football season! After I'm done Hi-Stepping for the year, I promise I'll be more reliable."

"Mmm-hmm. You might come back and find out somebody else done took your spot."

"You wouldn't do that, Mother."

She lets out her low and throaty laugh. "And why not?"

"Because you love me, that's why!"

"Humph! I also love my Lean Cuisines."

"I promise I'll be back, Mother Cranford!" I see Gwen waving at me from across the sanctuary. "My mom wants me right now, though, so I gotta run."

"All right, baby. Have a blessed week."

"You too, Mother."

Gwen has this huge smile on her face like she has something good to tell me. It must not be too good, because Candy is standing next to her and scowling hard.

"Hey, Mommy," I say to Gwen as I give her a hug.

Candy rolls her eyes. She better fall back, because I don't do all that eye-rolling when she's saying Daddy this and Daddy that.

"We're going to dinner with Pastor today, so I wanted to make sure you didn't get lost with your friends."

Dinner with Pastor Stokes is so not the business. The conversation is usually boring and Gwen always finds some reason to get offended. Typically, it's something that my aunt Elena says. But maybe Gwen will be cool today after just hearing a message about loving our enemies.

"Can I ride with Pastor?" I ask. I don't want to spend any extra time in close quarters with LeRon or with Candy's gloomy self.

"Sure. Go ahead."

I walk across the sanctuary to where Hope and Aunt Elena are sitting and waiting for Pastor Stokes. Umm . . . why is Hope frowning at me like she doesn't have good sense? Now I'm thinking I'd rather deal with gloomy Candy.

Before I even get a chance to say hello, Hope says, "I'm not speaking to you, Gia."

"What did I do this time?" I ask wearily.

"Kevin told me that you, he, and Ricky are all going to Homecoming together as a group."

What is wrong with Kevin? All that praying and carrying on, you'd think he'd have better sense than to tell this to Hope right after Ricky rejected her.

"Yeah, we talked about it a week ago, I guess. No big deal."

Hope's eyes watered. "A week ago? You knew you were going to Homecoming with Ricky a week ago and you still let me walk around thinking he was gonna go with me? Gia, you are foul for that."

"Wait a minute. *I* didn't let you do anything. Don't get mad at me because you wouldn't listen to anyone."

"But you knew I wanted to go with him and then you go and make plans behind my back?"

I let out a huge sigh. "Look, we're going as a group. We're not going *together* like on a date. If you weren't trying to make Ricky your boo we probably would've invited you too."

Aunt Elena, who had been paying us no attention up until now, gets into the conversation. "What is going on here? Hope, you know how your father and I feel about dating."

Hope nods. "Right. You have to know the boy and his parents, and it has to be in groups."

"Okay, as long as we're on the same page . . ."

"We are, Mom. You know Ricky's parents."

Aunt Elena's face lights up. "Ricardo Freeman? Little Ricky?"

I don't know where Aunt Elena has been, but Ricky is definitely not "Little Ricky" anymore.

"Yes, Ricky Freeman," Hope says, with a half smile.

Elena hugs Hope and kisses her on the cheek. "He's a wonderful young man. I'm happy you chose him. So what are you two fussing about?"

Okay . . . Twilight Zone alert. Is Hope gonna tell her mother that Ricky is one hundred percent against dating anyone?

Hope replies, "Gia and Kevin made plans to go with Ricky to Homecoming when they both knew I wanted to ask him."

"Aunt Elena, isn't the boy supposed to ask the girl?" I ask.

Elena takes a long pause. "Well, in a perfect world, the boy should do the pursuing. But sometimes they're shy and need a little prompting. It doesn't hurt for them to know you like them too."

"See, I told you, Gia," Hope says.

I throw up the *whatever* hand to Hope. "Auntie, what

if the boy says he doesn't like you? Are you supposed to keep chasing him and harassing his friends?"

Now Aunt Elena looks confused. "He doesn't like Hope? How could he not like Hope? She's flawless and honestly the best he can do in this church."

"Thank you, Mommy!" Hope says as she hugs her mother around the neck.

Remind me why I said I wanted to ride with them? I think I'll take doom and gloom over crazy and crazier! And what does Aunt Elena mean that Hope is the best Ricky can do in this church? Anyway!

Aunt Elena looks up at me from her hug. "Gia, I expect you to include your cousin on this group-date thing for Homecoming."

"It's not a date."

"Well, I still expect her to be invited. Your mother and I have that agreement, you know, that we won't allow either of you to leave the other out."

Yes, I know that Elena and Gwen said that many, many years ago. But I can't even count how many times they've broken that agreement over the years. I think all the sleepovers, birthday parties, and spa days that I've been left out of, entitle me to one cool night out with my best friend.

When I don't reply to my aunt's command, she says, "Did you hear what I said, Gia? All four of you have hung out together in the past . . . wait . . . there's Ricky now. Ricky! Come over here, please!"

Ricky is going to be extra salty. But he can't blame this on me. He can blame it on big mouth, church gossip, Kevin.

"Praise the Lord, First Lady Elena. Hey, Hope! Hey, Gia!" Ricky says with his typical chipper tone.

"Hello, Ricky," says Aunt Elena. "What's this I hear about you all not inviting Hope to be in your group for Homecoming?"

Ricky's eyes widen and he looks at me. I say one word. "Kevin."

"It wasn't done purposely, First Lady," Ricky explains. "We thought that Hope wanted to go with a boy on a date, and we didn't want to do that."

"Well, I think you should all go together! That would be the best thing," Aunt Elena says. "You're all friends anyway."

Hope has a triumphant look on her face because she must know, like I know, that there is no way Ricky can get out of this one. Ricky looks a little bit green, actually, like he's about to be sick.

"Okay, First Lady. Hope can come with us, as long as she knows that I'm *not* her date."

Hope glares angrily at Ricky and I cover my mouth to hold in my laughter. That's exactly what she gets for trying to put him on blast to her mama. Ha!

Aunt Elena is not pleased. "That's fine, Ricky. But you could do a lot worse than my Hope."

Why did she just look at me when she said that? Am I supposed to be "a lot worse"? Auntie must forget that I've got Gwen's blood running through my veins. She better be glad I'm trying not to embarrass my mother and that we're in the sanctuary.

"Oh, I know, First Lady. Hope is a great girl. I just don't think I'm ready for all that yet."

Aunt Elena sees Pastor Stokes walk out of his office and she stands. "Well, it's settled then. Hope will join the rest of you for Homecoming. I'm sure it'll be lovely. We're going out to dinner now, Ricky. Have a blessed week."

"You too, First Lady."

I try to walk away with my aunt and cousin, but Ricky grabs my arm and holds me back. He whispers, "What was *that* about?"

"Ask your boy Kevin! He's the one who told Hope our plan, and Aunt Elena doesn't like the idea that you might actually be rejecting her daughter."

"This is a mess! I don't want to walk into Homecoming with Hope! Everyone's gonna think we're *together*."

I nod in agreement. "Not to mention that if everyone thinks you and Hope are on a date, everyone's gonna assume that I'm with Kevin. Me definitely no likee."

"So you better think of something then, Gia."

Ricky runs off to talk to the youth choir director and I head out to the parking lot. Why does everything have to be up to me to fix? I'm not a miracle worker! But trust and believe I will not have anyone thinking that I'm with Kevin! Ewwww . . .

★ 25 ★

I'm sitting at the table finishing up my math homework for tomorrow. I know I waited until the last minute, but this weekend has been so action-packed that I'm just now getting around to it. It *would* consist of a bunch of story problems that I hate! Ugh!!!

LeRon is in the kitchen rummaging around in the refrigerator for something. I don't know what it could be, because he ate so much at dinner that I was embarrassed for him. As soon as Pastor Stokes said he was treating, LeRon started ordering stuff off the menu that he didn't even know how to pronounce. He knows good and well he wouldn't ever go up in a restaurant ordering roast duck. He needs to stop playing.

"What are you doing?" he asks.

"My math homework."

He nods. "You should've gotten that done before all of your fun."

"Yeah, I guess. But my mom lets me be responsible for how I get my work done, as long as it's done. I get straight A's, so I must be doing something right." I'm not about to let him stand up here and clown me, for real.

"Straight A's! You must be really proud of that."

Why is he trying to have a conversation with me? Does he not see me trying to finish my homework? I'm trying to be *responsible*. Good grief!

"Umm . . . yeah. I am. I need to get scholarships if I want to go to the college I choose."

"So where do you want to go?" he asks.

"Spelman, I think."

"All the way to Atlanta, huh?"

I put my pencil down and look at LeRon. If I send him a mental vibe or two that this isn't conversation time, maybe he'll let me finish this. I've got eight story problems to go, because the first four took an hour. I don't want to be up all night long!

LeRon swallows a bite out of the huge hunk of cake he's holding. "Oh, I'm sorry. You're trying to get your work done."

"It's okay. I'll . . . ummm . . . let you get back to your cake now." Okay, this is really awkward.

"All right. See you in the morning," LeRon says and then starts toward his and Gwen's bedroom with his cake and a glass of milk.

Good! Go to bed, man!

"Umm, Gia?"

Grrr! What now? "Yes?"

"I just wanted to say that I'm sorry for how I've been treating you."

Huh? Okay, totally did not expect this.

"It's okay," I reply.

"No. It's not okay. Your mother has gone out of her way to make sure Candy feels welcome in this family, and I haven't extended you the same courtesy."

I take a huge gulp. How am I supposed to respond to this? *Am* I supposed to respond to this?

"I forgive you, LeRon."

"Well, thanks. But I want to prove what I'm saying, Gia. I've decided to set up a little office in the corner of the living room so you can have the other bedroom. You're used to your own space, and it's not right that you have to share with Candy. How about you, your mother, and I go and pick out paint and decorations for your new room?"

"Thank you, LeRon!"

I am so excited, I can almost give him a hug. I said *almost*. It's a process, people.

"You're welcome, Gia. Good night."

"Good night."

Well, who saw this one coming? Definitely not me! I guess that's how God works, though. Sometimes He does things for you when you least expect it.

So what color should my new room be? I'm thinking Tweety yellow . . .

★ 26 ★

"**G**ia, hide me!"
Why is Candy convinced that she can go through the entire school day without someone peeping out her ri-darn-diculous outfit? She plans to wear her winter coat all day?

"Candy, you need to take that coat off and put it in your locker," I say as she darts behind my locker door. A group of cheerleaders are walking down the hall.

"No! If we do this properly, no one has to know about this."

Kevin and Ricky are coming toward us, because we usually walk to breakfast together.

"Oh, no!" Candy whines. "Tell them to go away!"

"I will not. You are not going to make me be a part of your punishment, Candy. You're just gonna have to suck it up!"

Kevin is the first one to notice Candy's lame gear. "What in the world are you wearing?" he asks.

Now, you know your outfit is looking crazy if tight-Wrangler-and-patent-leather-church-shoe boy is clowning you. Dang!

Ricky throws his head back and laughs. "Gwen is off the charts! I can't believe she's got you looking this foolish."

"Don't blame this all on Gwen. Her daddy was in on this too!" I exclaim. "I actually think it was his idea."

Candy's eyes drop to the floor. "I didn't think y'all would laugh at me too!" she says.

"Okay, okay. We're sorry," Kevin says. "This will be our one and only time laughing at your . . . ensemble."

Valerie is marching down the hall with her minions, because today is the day we vote for Homecoming court. She's handing out brownies with her picture on them, to remind people to vote for her. Ricky, on the other hand, is wearing a *Romeo for Prince* button to remind people *not* to vote for him!

Hilarious.

Of course, Valerie stops at our little crew and hands everyone a brownie. She stops at Candy.

"Oh my goodness," Valerie says as she looks Candy up and down. "Please tell me that is a Halloween costume of some sort. Who are you supposed to be?"

Candy mumbles, "It's not a costume."

"What did you say, chica? I didn't hear you. Did you say that this eyesore of an outfit is *not* a costume?"

Candy takes a deep breath and points her chin up.

"No. It is not a costume. It's what I'll be wearing for a while."

"What? Have you lost your mind? Hi-Steppers don't roll like that." Valerie looks like she's about ready to faint.

"I know, right?" Kelani chirps. "Those pants are not the business."

Jewel adds, "And those shoes, mami! What are you thinking?"

Okay, since when did Jewel start with the Latina jargon? It's sooo not cute.

"Are you three finished?" Ricky asks.

Valerie's face turns into a twisted frown. Candy's eyes widen with panic. "It's cool, Valerie! It's just a dare that I lost to Gia. Right, Gia?"

She's looking at me with pleading eyes, but I am not about to lie for her, so I don't say anything.

Valerie seems skeptical. "Mmm-hmm. So why weren't you at my hayride on Saturday?"

"Umm . . . I-I wasn't feeling well." So I guess she's just gonna keep lying, huh? She hasn't learned her lesson at all.

Valerie hands her box of brownies to Jewel and gets right in Candy's face. "I think you're lying. You don't do it well, honey. Now, what's really going on?"

Candy takes a long, deep breath. I don't think she wanted to spill her guts about this punishment thing, but Valerie is not gonna stop until she gets the truth.

"I'm on punishment," Candy says.

"For what? What could you have done that would be sooo bad that your parents would make you wear this?" Valerie's hand sweeps the air up and down Candy's gear.

Then, something apparently clicks in Valerie's head. "Did you get caught shoplifting?"

Candy doesn't answer. She just looks away.

"Oooh! Your parents are dead wrong for this!" Kelani says.

Valerie puts a hand up to shush Kelani. "So how long is this going to go on?"

"A month," Candy replies in a voice barely above a whisper.

"A month! This is not good. We're going to have to evaluate your A-squad status if you're going to be looking like an idiot for a whole month."

I have to cut in. "Okay, Valerie. That's enough. I think she already feels bad as it is, you don't have to rub it in. Plus, she's only allowed to come to practice during her punishment, not perform."

Valerie frowns. "So your actions are going to cause a hole in the Hi-Steppers line? This is completely unacceptable. This is grounds for removal from the squad."

"Chill out, Valerie. She's not being kicked off the squad for this," I say matter-of-factly.

"Says who?" Valerie asks with mucho attitude.

"Says me. As co-captain of the squad, I have just as much say as you do."

"We'll see about that."

Kevin says, "Valerie, why don't you go and hand out the rest of your little brownies now?"

Valerie flares her nose in Kevin's direction. "Are you trying to dismiss me? Lames cannot dismiss me."

"I wasn't trying to dismiss you, Valerie, but I do think you're done here."

"Don't get it twisted!" Valerie huffs, snatches her brownies from Jewel, and marches down the hallway.

Everyone else, including Jewel and Kelani, look at Kevin. We all have admiration in our eyes. Did he just stand up to Valerie and totally dismiss her? Wow!

Maybe Kevin really is changing.

In homeroom, we get the Homecoming court ballots and have to cast our votes. I scan down the page to see who's running. The only ones I really know on the ballot are Valerie, Ricky, and Romeo.

I go ahead and mark Valerie's name, because aside from her foolishness, I really think she deserves it. I'm torn when it comes to Ricky and Romeo, though. I know Ricky really doesn't want to be prince, but there is no way in the world I can vote for Romeo.

So, I leave it blank.

Jewel collects the ballots and, of course, she reads every single one of them. Has she ever heard of the term "secret ballot"?

When she gets to my desk, she quickly reads over my choices. "Why didn't you vote for Ricky?" she asks.

"Because he doesn't want to be the Homecoming prince."

Jewel shakes her head and frowns. "He is so weird. Why didn't he just withdraw his name from the ballot?"

"He didn't want to hurt the feelings of whoever nominated him."

"Oh. Well, don't you know that it was your cousin who nominated him? I heard she was gonna run for princess too, but then she chickened out."

Hmmm . . . that's interesting. I had no idea how desperate Hope was to date Ricky. She's resorted to all kinds of foolishness just to get that boy's attention.

"I hope Ricky doesn't find out it was her, because he'd be pretty salty," I say.

"Well, I voted for him and I hope he wins! I can't stand Romeo. He's sooo conceited."

Umm . . . yeah. This is information that I already know. But I think Jewel is just a little bit heated that Romeo's with Valerie now. She'd put in some work on him after he played me like a dummy, and he pretty much ignored her.

"So, I figured out a way to let everyone know that Hope is not your date at Homecoming," I say to Ricky as we sit at the lunch table.

"Cool! Spill it."

"Well, we can . . . wait a minute. Kevin, what are you eating?"

Kevin swallows a huge bite. "Egg salad on white bread."

"Good grief, Kevin. We are not in third grade! I'm gonna need you to upgrade your lunch food."

"What? I like egg salad. The way Granny makes it, it's sweet and savory at the same time!"

I throw a napkin at Kevin. "You're relapsing, Kevin! Resist the inner corny. Please!"

"Gia, leave Kev alone and tell me your plan," Ricky says.

"How do you feel about a dance step and matching outfits?"

Ricky bursts out laughing. "Umm . . . about the same way you feel about egg salad sandwiches."

"No, seriously! Think about it. If you, Kevin, and I come dressed similarly and we do a dance step together, it kind of makes Hope look like she's tagging along."

"One problem," Kevin says. "I don't know how to dance."

"Well, Ricky and I will do most of the dancing. You'll just be our hype man."

"What's a hype man?" Kevin asks.

"Seriously, Kev," Ricky replies. "It's like how Flavor Flav was to the rest of Public Enemy."

Kevin frowns. "Flavor Flav? Do I have to wear a clock?"

"No, Kev! You just get the crowd pumped as we dance."

Kevin still doesn't look agreeable. I think we lost him as soon as we said Flavor Flav.

"What kind of outfit?"

"I'm thinking a mixture of jeans and Tweety."

"No way I'm wearing Tweety, Gia. Forget it," Ricky says.

"Okay, how about jeans and orange tops?" I ask.

Ricky calms down a little. "I'm listening. Would you wear a T-shirt?"

"No, I have a fitted orange blouse. It'll actually be pretty cute."

Kevin asks, "Aren't girls supposed to wear nice dresses at Homecoming?"

I shrug. "I don't know. I've never been. But I'll accessorize. Is that all right with you, Kev?"

"Gia, everything you say is pretty much all right with me," Kevin replies as he takes another bite of his sandwich.

Ricky and I stare at Kevin in shock. This is the second time today that he's caught us off guard. I thought he was cured of his crush on me, but I guess he was only in remission.

★ 27 ★

"Did you hear?" Hope asks.

Okay, I'm not exactly speaking to Hope right now, but she doesn't know it. I'm really irritated how she used her pastor's-daughter status to muscle her way into our Homecoming crew. That was the opposite of cool.

I roll my eyes. "Did I hear what, Hope?"

"What's wrong with you?" she asks—I guess hearing how annoyed I sound.

"Nothing."

She narrows her eyes. "Are you mad because I'm coming with you guys to Homecoming?"

"What do you think?"

"Why would you be mad? It's not like it's a date!"

"You're right. It's not a date."

Okay, I have sooo had it with her. "Whatever, Hope! I've got to go to Hi-Steppers rehearsal. What did you want to tell me?"

"Oh, just that Susan beat Valerie for Homecoming queen."

My mouth falls open. "You're joking."

"Nope. I heard she won by a landslide too. They're gonna announce it in the morning."

Valerie losing to Susan is pretty much the worst thing that could happen to the Hi-Steppers a week before Homecoming. It's going to be all bad. I'm putting her on Kevin's and Mother Cranford's prayer lists and the Hi-Stepper squad's too.

I can hear her screaming before I even walk into the locker room.

"How did this *happen*?" Valerie wails.

Kelani hugs Valerie tightly. "We all voted for you, Valerie."

"Well, then *who* voted for Susan?"

I wonder if Valerie realizes just how many people don't like her. She's spent every school year terrorizing people she felt were beneath her. I'm thinking that maybe *only* the Hi-Steppers voted for her.

"I can't believe these people would come to my party, eat my food, and *not* vote for me!"

"That's bananas, Valerie," Jewel says. "But at least you're still going to Homecoming with Romeo."

"No, I'm not. He only wanted to be my date if I won! He won prince, and said that he needs to go to Homecoming with a princess."

Candy quickly changes out of her prison clothing into her Hi-Steppers practice gear, and tries not to make eye contact with Valerie. But it doesn't work.

"What about you, Candy? Did you vote for me?" Valerie asks.

"Of course I did."

Valerie balls her fists at her side and starts punching her own thigh. "Everyone keeps saying that they voted for me, but someone is lying! If I had all these votes, I'd be Homecoming queen! But I'm not. Susan is going to be on the field, in that float, wearing *my* crown."

Karma is such a mean girl.

Next Valerie does something I've never heard her do. She's muttering in Spanish. Real Spanish. Not one *chica* is heard. You would need subtitles to understand what she's saying. Who knew she was really bilingual?

Out in the gym, Mrs. Vaughn blows her whistle, so even though Valerie is still spazzing out, the rest of the Hi-Steppers leave the locker room. We have to finalize our Homecoming-game routine, so Valerie has to get over her temper tantrum real quick.

"Let's warm up, ladies!"

Jewel comes over to stretch with me and whispers, "Can you believe how Valerie is tripping?"

"Yeah, it's crazy. But what about Romeo? That's foul that he's ditching her. I thought she had dirt on him."

"She does, or did, anyway."

"Did?"

Jewel whispers, "Well, Valerie helped Romeo buy some papers for his English class."

"For real? Where did she get them?"

"She's got a hookup with someone she met online," Jewel explains. "He was failing and Coach Rogers wasn't gonna let him play."

"Oh."

"But he's not in the class anymore, so he's not thinking about Valerie!"

Mrs. Vaughn yells, "Does anyone know where Valerie is? We've got a Homecoming routine to choreograph!"

"She's in the locker room having a meltdown because she didn't win the Homecoming queen title."

"Gia, go in there and get Valerie. Tell her if she doesn't want to lose another title, then she better hustle herself on out here immediately."

Dang! Why did Mrs. Vaughn have to send me? I'm no good at this comforting thing, especially with someone like Valerie.

When I walk into the locker room, Valerie is sitting on the floor with her knees pulled up to her chest. She's sobbing into her hands, and her entire body is shaking. Trust me, it's a pitiful sight . . . all bad.

"Valerie," I say quietly, "Mrs. Vaughn wants you to come out and rehearse for the game."

"The Homecoming game? There's no way I'm stepping on Friday. I can't step while Susan is on the field wearing my crown."

I sit down on the floor next to Valerie. "You know it's really not that serious, Valerie. For real, Homecoming is, like, one night."

"It's not that serious to you, Gia. But I've wanted this since ninth grade."

I bite my lip, trying to think of a different argument. "Are you going to let everyone see you twisted like this? I mean, I bet people didn't vote for you just because they wanted to see you lose it."

"Whatever, Gia. They didn't vote because they're haters."

"Well, my mother says that if you have haters then you must be doing something right."

Valerie chuckles. "Your mom is a lame, Gia."

"She is *not*!"

"I'm joking, chica."

"Don't make me hurt you."

Valerie stands. "So, I guess we should go to practice, huh?"

"Unless you plan to let the haters win."

"Umm, no, never that."

As we head back to the gym, a thought occurs to me. "Valerie, do you want to ride with us to Homecoming?"

"Who are you going with?"

"Kevin, Hope, and Ricky."

Valerie scrunches her nose. "Do you think they'd mind me coming? It sounds like a double date."

"It is sooo not a double date! You let me handle everybody else. You just be ready when we pick you up."

"No way, Gia."

I just told Ricky about inviting Valerie to come to Homecoming with us and this is the reaction that I get. He is so not being a Christian about this.

"What would Jesus do, Ricky?" I ask as I start our dance step again.

Kevin, who is sitting on my living room couch, lets out a petite giggle. Yeah, it was petite, and unwelcome. I'm gonna need him to not laugh when I'm trying to make a serious point.

"Jesus would lead me not into temptation but deliver me from evil," Ricky replies.

Oh no, he didn't come at me with the Lord's Prayer. That's what I get for sparring with a church kid.

"Ricky!"

"No, Gia. I'm putting my foot down. It's my car."

I narrow my eyes angrily. "Okay, well if you are too mean to take Valerie, then I'm not going."

"Gia, if you don't want to go with him, I can drive," Keven says. "I'll pick you up in my grandfather's Cadillac."

I vote no to Kevin and the rusty Cadi. He's been trying to get me in that car ever since he got his driver's license.

But for the sake of argument I say, "Cool, Kev. It's on then. Pick me up at six on Saturday."

"Cool!" The way Kevin's eyes light up is definitely not the business.

"Wait a minute," Ricky says. "That leaves me alone with Hope."

I reply, "Sounds like a date to me."

"It sure does!" Kevin says. "If you had wanted to be alone with Hope, all you had to do was tell us."

Kevin and I burst into laughter and share a high-five. Ricky scowls at both of us and sits down on the couch.

"I won't go alone with Hope. I just won't go at all. How about that?"

I can feel the smile creeping up on my face. I've got him exactly where I want him, but he doesn't even know it.

"You could stay at home, but how do you think the rest of the football team would feel if the starting quarterback just didn't show up at the Homecoming dance?"

Ricky frowns and I guess that he's considering his options. After a few moments, he gets up and walks over to the CD player. He presses Play, and Ne-Yo's "Closer" blares from the speakers.

"Well?" Ricky asks.

"Well what?"

"Are we making up a step or not?"

Now the smile blooms across my face. "We're still making up our step? Does that mean you're going?"

Ricky nods.

"Are we taking Valerie too?"

Ricky nods again. I jump and hug Ricky around his neck. "Thank you, Ricky! You won't regret it, I promise."

"I'm sure I will," Ricky replies.

★ 28 ★

The Homecoming game is so not a pretty sight for Valerie. She's trying her hardest to not look pressed, stressed, or twisted that she's not a part of the Homecoming court. She's coming up miserably short.

Valerie and I stand in the front row of the bleachers, pretending to cheer for Ricky and the rest of the Spartans. It's not like they need our cheers, though. They are crushing the Normandy Eagles.

Valerie halts all clapping and cheering when Romeo runs a catch in for a touchdown. The hate in her eyes is really ridiculous. I mean, I was extra salty when he left me at the beach, but I know I didn't have this kind of anger.

She needs to do what Mother Cranford says and lay it on the altar. That means that sometimes people do things or things happen that are so bad that you can't do anything else but tell God about it and let Him handle it. That's what Valerie needs to do, for real.

Valerie jumps when I place my hand on her back. "What?" she asks.

"Nothing. Are you okay?"

She smiles wickedly. "Of course I'm okay."

I don't like the look on her face. I mean, she's looking super sick right now. "I'm serious, Valerie."

"I am too." Valerie folds her arms and raises one eyebrow. Now I know she's up to something.

"Valerie, whatever you're planning, don't do it. It's not worth it."

"Gia, you're such a good girl, you really are. But that isn't me. I can't operate being the goody-goody."

Okay . . . whatever. She's got me standing up here sounding like a straight-up preacher's kid. If she wants to make a fool of herself doing whatever she has planned, then that's her business. I can't be Captain Save-a-Chica every time.

And can you believe she called me a goody-goody. Eh . . . no!

Since it's not quite time for us to line up for the half-time show, I walk over to where my mom, LeRon, and Candy are sitting. The only reason they let her come to the game is because LeRon didn't trust her to be at home by herself.

That's completely tragic that they don't trust her, but on the upside, they didn't make her wear the prison clothes to the game.

Gwen calls Candy's punishment outfit "prison clothes,"

because, in her words, *Honey, you only get one outfit when you go to prison and that's where you're headed if you keep taking things that don't belong to you.*

"Hi, Mom!" I say as I lean into the row to give Gwen a kiss on the cheek.

"Hey, Gia."

"Hi, Candy. Hi, LeRon."

LeRon says, "Gia, shouldn't you be down there with the squad?"

"I will in a minute, but I wanted to come and say hi."

Candy doesn't say anything to me. I guess she's heated about being on punishment.

"Hey, *Candy*!" I say her name extra loud so she can't ignore me.

"It's bad enough that I have to be here with the parental units. Don't expect me to be happy about it," Candy replies and then turns her head back to the action on the field.

Gwen asks, "Where's Hope? Is she here tonight?"

I point over in the direction of the rally girls. They are super hyped tonight because of Susan's Homecoming victory. They're all wearing red velour track suits, looking like they're on their way to yoga class or something.

Gwen waves over at Hope. "Well, it looks like she's having fun."

"I'm sure she is, Mom. I have to go back with the Hi-Steppers. See you after IHOP."

"Don't stay out past curfew, Gia, or you will not be attending the dance tomorrow night."

"Okay, Mom. Gotcha!"

Umm, seriously, I think Gwen got all hardcore right then,

for LeRon and Candy's benefit. Because first and foremost, I'm never late for curfew. On the real, I'm always about ten to fifteen minutes early. I know Gwen isn't playing on that. And second, there is no way I'm doing anything to get me grounded before Homecoming. I missed it last year because I was on some foolish stuff with Romeo.

Right before we get ready to march onto the field Hope jogs up to the Hi-Steppers' line. I can't think of anything that she would want, other than to rub Valerie's face in her defeat. That is not cool, even if Valerie owns the title of mean girl.

"Hey, Gia. What are you wearing tomorrow?" Hope asks.

Okay, seriously. Is that the best thing she could come up with? "A blouse and some jeans probably. Why?" I say. Of course, I fail to mention my color coding with Kevin and Ricky.

"Well, because I wanted to see if you wanted us to dress similar or something. Not alike, but just similar."

I watch Valerie's shoulders shake up and down in silent laughter. She's standing directly in front of me in the Hi-Steppers' line, so there is no way that she can hide her inner giggles.

"What is so funny, Valerie?" I ask.

"Nothing, except that dressing like twins went out in, like, 2002. So completely and utterly lame. I can't believe I'm rolling with y'all to Homecoming."

I bite my lip because I don't want to have this conversation right now. I've got to get my head in the game and remember the step, so I'm truly not trying to have an argument with Hope.

But, of course, it looks like she has other ideas.

"Is this true, Gia? Is Valerie going with us? Since when?"

"Yes, yes, and since two days ago," I reply. "Any more questions?"

Hope crosses her arms and narrows her eyes in Valerie's direction. "I won't go anywhere with her."

"Suit yourself," Valerie says with a chuckle. "Then I won't have to worry about you trying to ride shotgun with Rick."

Hope's lips form a tight little O. "You are soooo not riding shotgun with Ricky."

I respond, "Well, I guess you have to go with us to keep that from happening, right? Plus, I thought we were clear on the whole *not a date* thing. Who cares who rides shotgun with Ricky? It doesn't mean anything."

Hope sneers angrily in Valerie's direction. "If I can't have him, then you definitely can't have him!"

"Boo, you don't tell me who I can and cannot have! Anyway, I don't *want* Ricky. I was just messing with you. It's obvious that he and Gia like each other, and Hi-Steppers don't share boys."

Hope looks from me to Valerie and storms away. Why do they have to keep making this about me and Ricky? It's like they're both trying to force the issue of Ricky and me getting together. If it's gonna happen, it'll happen, but dang, we don't need any help. Especially not from certified haters!

As we get ready to march onto the field, I watch Valerie pull Kelani by the arm and say, "Are you ready, chica?"

Kelani nods grimly, like she doesn't appreciate what Valerie said. It kind of reminds me of when a teacher asks you if you're ready for a test, and you aren't *really* ready, but you can't say no because it's the teacher.

"What's going on?" I ask loud enough for both of them to hear me.

Valerie replies, "Nothing. I'm talking about the step. What did you think I was talking about?"

Before we march onto the field, the Homecoming court rides across the field on floats made by the rally girls and the Student Council. The decorations are decent, but seriously, those floats look hazardous. They couldn't pay me to ride on one of them.

As the floats make their last lap around the field, the Hi-Steppers follow the marching band out to the fifty-yard line. Since it's Homecoming, we are stepping to the school song. I know it's boring, but it's a tradition.

Immediately, I can tell that something is off with Valerie, because she's not even attempting to do our step. She's marching forward, separating herself from the rest of the Hi-Steppers. At the end of the school song, she pulls something out of her pocket.

It's a whistle.

She blows three times on the whistle and the band stops playing. The drum major throws his baton into the air and as he catches it he points at Valerie. Her back is to us, but I can almost guarantee she's smiling.

After a long pause—long enough for everyone in the

bleachers to stare down at the field—Kelani runs over to the drum major and takes the cape and top hat from his outstretched hands.

Okay, what's really going on?

Next Kelani places the hat on Valerie's head and drapes the cape over Valerie's shoulders.

The drum major takes his megaphone and shouts to the band. "Who's the real queen of Longfellow High?"

"VALERIE!" the band shouts in unison.

"I can't hear you!"

"VALERIE!"

The drum major yells, "Spell it OUT!"

"V-A-L-E-R-I-E!" The drummers pound the snare drums with each letter.

I'm convinced that Valerie has lost her entire mind. If I needed any more proof, she gives it to me by strutting across the field, waving that cape from side to side. No one in the bleachers claps or cheers. In fact, some of them boo, but I guess Valerie doesn't need their approval.

After she's done showing off, Valerie marches off the field with the rest of the Hi-Steppers and the band behind her. Mrs. Vaughn is not one of Valerie's fans, because she snatches the cape from Valerie's shoulders.

When we're seated in the bleachers I ask, "Valerie, how did you get the drum major to go along with that?"

Valerie laughs. "Gia, I thought you knew me! I happen to be irresistible to boys, chica. It was actually pretty easy. I told him I'd go to the Homecoming dance with him."

"So you're not going with us now? Why did you mess with Hope then, if you knew you weren't coming with us?"

"Well, I had to make sure everything went down as planned before I cancelled my plans with you guys." Valerie gives me a weak smile. "Truthfully, though, your friends aren't really my cup of tea."

"Since when? You were just trying to holla at Ricky a few weeks ago."

"That was before I realized he was truly a lame. And that Kevin . . . Gia, you can't expect me to show up anywhere with him."

This time I laugh. "Okay, I'll give you that. Kevin is a bit extra. But he's one of my best friends, so I can't let you talk bad about him."

Mrs. Vaughn glares at us from the field. "You better hope you're irresistible to Mrs. Vaughn too!" I say. "She looks like she's about to explode."

"She'll be all right," Valerie replies. "Plus, it was totally worth it!"

I will say this about Valerie; she definitely goes after what she wants. Sometimes she gets it and sometimes she doesn't, but she never sits on the side waiting for someone else to do something.

Out of all her qualities, this is the only one I actually admire. Go figure.

"Gia . . ." Valerie says.

"Yes?"

"I didn't get to really thank you for inviting me to Homecoming with you guys. That was cool of you, and you didn't have to do it."

"It was nothing!"

"Well, thanks anyway."

Mrs. Vaughn walks toward us and Valerie jumps to her feet. "Tell her I had to go to the bathroom!"

"Okay," I reply with a giggle.

Now who would've thought that Valerie would appreciate a random act of kindness?

★ 29 ★

It's Saturday, and of course, the Homecoming dance is today. Yay! My first high school Homecoming dance. I was banned from attending during my freshman year, and last year there was a series of unfortunate events.

But this year, I'm going and I'm going to be extra fresh, extra clean, and supa dupa fly!

Gwen and I are sitting at the dining room table in chill mode. LeRon took Candy out for a father-daughter breakfast. I guess they needed some bonding time. Whatever. I'm just glad to have them out of the house.

I'm also glad that Gwen didn't try to force any of those grits on me. I don't think that grits are supposed to be a solid, shiny lump. They look like a special effect from a horror movie, especially the way Gwen is stabbing them with a fork.

"So, Homecoming is tonight, right?" Gwen asks. "What are you wearing?"

"Ricky, Kevin, and I are wearing orange tops and blue jeans."

Gwen scrunches her nose. "Jeans at Homecoming?"

"Yeah, Mom. It's not really a formal thing at our school. Everyone dresses kinda casually."

"If that's what you want, I guess it's okay. Have you thought about how you want to decorate your new room? LeRon is really excited about shopping for your furniture."

"I haven't really had a chance to think about it."

"Well, don't wait too long! You better get it while the getting is good."

"Okay, got it."

Gwen smiles at me. "With LeRon and Candy out of the house, doesn't this feel like old times?"

"Yeah, it does."

"As happy as I am to be married to LeRon, I do miss our alone time."

There's no way she can miss it more than I do. At least she got a husband out of the deal. All I got was extra roommates.

"Mom, sometimes I wish we could go back to the way it was."

"Life is all about change, Gia. Like Kevin, for instance . . . he's changing, right?"

I burst out laughing. "How did this conversation get to be about Kevin?"

"I'm just making a point," Gwen replies, joining in on my laughter. "I noticed that Kevin is trying to come out of his shell."

"I don't know about that, but he's gonna be me and Ricky's hype man tonight at the dance."

Gwen covers her mouth, trying to hold in her laughter. "Hype man? Does he even know what a hype man is?"

"No! We had to tell him!"

My mom and I are both laughing so hard that we're bent over and holding our stomachs. This is what I really miss. How much fun we used to have when we lived in our little duplex. Even when I was in trouble or on punishment, and even when she was chasing after some guy, we still had some great times.

I really miss that.

"You know, Gia, sometimes changes are for the better."

I nod slowly. I agree that everything around me has definitely changed, but the jury is still out on if our life is better.

Candy watches me as I stand in front of the mirror in our bedroom. I'm trying to make a perfect bow with the tie on my orange blouse. It's not a really bright orange, but more the color of leaves in the fall. In addition to the bow, the collar has ruffles. It's fierce and casual at the same time. And of course my skinny jeans and ankle boots are banging.

Yes, I am totally feeling myself right about now. Deal with it.

"Your blouse is cute," Candy says.

"Thanks."

"I wish I was going with you guys," Candy says wistfully. "I saw the step you and Ricky are gonna do. It's hot!"

"If you keep your nose clean, you can kick it with us next year!"

"Next year? How about the Winter Ball, the Valentine's Day dance, Spring Fling, and prom?"

I laugh out loud. "The prom? Who in the world is asking you to the prom? Did you forget that you are a freshman, boo?"

"Don't underestimate me! I could probably get a prom date before you do!"

I'm not going to argue with her because number one, she might be right, and number two, Gwen has a rule. No prom unless you're graduating.

I can hear Ricky, Hope, and Kevin's voices from the living room.

"Well, my ride is here. You wanna come out of your prison cell and say hi?"

"Sure, why not," Candy says.

Mmm . . . kay, did I just step out of my bedroom and into the Twilight Zone? Can I just say—and it's hard for me to say this without flinching—that Kevin looks extraordinarily fly.

I'm not talking just a little change here or there. I'm talking major fashion overhaul. He has on some perfectly loose jeans with a rusty orange button-down shirt. He's also got on a jean jacket and, hold up, some tan Timberland boots.

"Kevin, boy, you look *good*." Candy voices my opinion.

And no, he does not have the audacity to blush. "Thanks, Candy."

Hope grins. "He does, doesn't he?"

Hope's outfit is very, very . . . umm . . . 90210. She's got on a silver dress with puffy sleeves and some black patent leather Mary Janes. I'm not feeling it, but it's all good, I guess.

"Well, what about me?" Ricky asks.

Ricky looks nice too, but then he always looks nice. His outfit is similar to Kevin's except he layered his blue button-down with an orange T-shirt underneath. He's got a new accessory, too. It's a fly silver chain that he's wearing around his neck.

"When did you start sporting silver?" I ask.

Ricky's hand self-consciously goes to his neck. "Oh, this? My mom gave this to me. Do you like it?"

I nod. "It's fresh, Ricky. Kev, you look great too."

"Thanks, Gia. You look really pretty," Kevin replies.

Gwen seems somewhat uncomfortable with this whole scene. Maybe it has something to do with how grown up we all are starting to look, even Kevin.

Ricky reaches into his pocket and pulls out a little box. "Gia, me and my mom saw this at the mall, and my mom said you would like it."

My eyes widen (Gwen and Hope's do too). I take the box from Ricky's hand and open it slowly. I can feel everyone's eyes on me, and Ricky's huge, proud smile.

In the box is a little silver charm bracelet with a Tweety charm. I can't contain my happiness. "Mom, put it on me! Thank you, Ricky!"

The gigantic hug that I give Ricky happens completely by accident. And he's going to need a napkin to wipe my lip gloss off his cheek. Yeah, that was unplanned as well . . . completely accidental.

"You're welcome, Gi-Gi. I know Tweety is on hiatus, but I thought you'd like to have him at your first Homecoming dance."

Hope frowns. "That is so sweet, Ricky." Okay, why do her words not match that crazy look on her face?

Kevin also looks a little twisted. He is sooo giving Ricky the how-dare-you-one-up-my-makeover side eye.

"Wait a minute!" Hope shouts.

Could she be any louder? Good grief!

"What?" I ask.

"Why are all three of you wearing orange?"

Candy giggles. "Did you not get the memo?"

"Was this on purpose?" Hope screeches at the top of her lungs.

Ricky replies, "Yes, it was planned."

"And you all conveniently forgot to tell me?"

Since I feel completely justified in our deception, I respond. "We just didn't want it to feel like a double date, Hope. It wasn't anything personal."

But how about the fact that this *does* feel like a date? Not a double date, but a Ricky-and-Gia date. A let-me-give-you-a-gift-before-we-go kind of date.

Ricky just gave me jewelry. My best and totally hot friend, who is a boy, just gave me jewelry. I'm trying not to let anyone in the room see how twisted I am about this, but I bet they can hear my heart beating because it's about to burst right out of my chest.

Why did I have to taint this moment? I should've waited

on Ricky to discover his true feelings before I detoured down a horrible road named Romeo.

Gwen pulls Hope into a one-armed hug. "But you all are still friends, right?"

"Of course!" I reply. "Dance steps just look hotter if you're wearing the same colors."

"You guys made up a dance step? Ugh! I can't stand y'all."

Kevin says, "Hope, you know you can't dance like Ricky and Gia."

"You can't either, Kevin! What are you gonna be doing?" Hope asks.

"I'm the hyper man."

Hyper man? Oh, good grief. You can take the lame out of his clothes, but you can't take the lame out of the boy!

★ 30 ★

I don't know why I feel ridiculously nervous walking into this Homecoming dance. It's not like super special or anything. Maybe I'm still excited about the little piece of jewelry on my wrist.

I mean, I know it's just Ricky, and he doesn't think he's feeling me or anybody else on that level, but could he kind of, subconsciously, like me? I mean *like* like me. You know. Because that would be really, really cool, but really, really scary at the same time.

All the way to the dance, I've been thinking that maybe I missed some clues about Ricky. Like when last year he was mad about me dating Romeo. Was he just blocking because Romeo was a dog, or was he *feeling* me? And like this year, when he refused to go to Homecoming with Valerie or Hope. Was that just because he's not trying to date anybody, or was it because he likes me and didn't want to say anything? Or what if he hasn't said anything because of Kevin's undying love for me, or Hope's crush?

So many questions! And I have absolutely no answers.

It's not like it would be completely out of the question. Because I would sooo definitely holla at him. If Ricky was my first real boyfriend—I refuse to count Romeo—that would be completely awesome. What's not to like? He's fine and sweet, he plays football, he's college bound! Okay, lemme fall back with all that. I don't want to go off on some crazy crush spree when there's no real evidence that my crush will be returned.

"What is up with you and Ricky?" Hope asks when the boys go and get us some snacks.

"Nothing. I love the way the rally girls decorated the gym. It totally doesn't look lame at all." Is it obvious that I'm trying to change the subject?

"Quit playing, Gia. You are not getting off that easy. Boys don't buy jewelry for girls unless they like them."

"Honestly, Hope . . . I don't know what's up. Ricky caught me off guard with that one too. What do you think about it? It's weird, huh?"

"Well, like I said before, you and Ricky are perfect for each other. I think he likes you. Maybe he doesn't know it yet, but he likes you."

"So, if he did *like* me, and I'm not saying that he does, but *if* he does, would you be angry if I talked to him?"

Hope sighs. "I might be a little jealous . . . okay, a lot jealous."

"Oh." This might be complicated.

"But I would get over it. It's always been you and Ricky. Seriously."

I don't believe her.

"It's not gonna happen, Hope, so it doesn't even matter."

A little smile dances on Hope's face. "Okay, but when it *does* happen, I really, really won't be mad forever, just for a few days . . . okay, weeks."

I refuse to respond to Hope's comment, because Ricky and Kevin are back with the snacks. So why do both of them try to hand me a cup of juice? Kevin frowns, and Hope takes the cup from Kevin's hand and grins.

Never, ever have I been more happy to see Valerie. She is so crazy, though. Why is she walking around with a tiara on and a pink dress? The word for the day, boys and girls, is *loca!*

"Ooo-OOO! Hey, Hi-Stepper!" Valerie says. And then she kisses my cheek. I really think she's lost it now.

"Hey, Valerie . . . cute crown."

Valerie smiles and touches her tiara. "Thank you! My mom bought it for me when I told her these losers didn't pick me for Homecoming queen."

"I see you didn't let that stop your reign," I reply.

"My rain? Gia, what are you talking about? Is it supposed to rain later? Thanks for telling me, because I don't think this tiara is real. I don't want it to rust."

I grab my forehead and shake my head back and forth. "Not that kind of rain, Valerie. *Reign,* like what a king does over his subjects."

I'm totally getting the blank stare from Valerie. She's getting a membership to the Sylvan Learning Center for her next birthday.

Valerie looks me up and down and scans my outfit. "I

see you, mami! You are looking very trendy. That bow is hot!"

"Thanks, Val."

Next Valerie checks Hope out. "And look at you, looking like a Disney princess."

"Ha, ha, Valerie."

Valerie completely disses Kevin and Ricky by pretending that they aren't even there. They don't seem to care. We all struggle not to laugh when Valerie walks away humming the theme song to *Mulan*.

"I can't stand her," Hope says in a huff.

"Your dress is nice," I say. "Don't let Valerie get to you."

"Whatever! I'm going over there with the rally girls. You three are making me stand out more with those jack-o-lantern shirts on."

As Hope storms away, our laughter continues. "Should I tell the DJ to play your song?" Kevin asks.

"Kev, trust, they are gonna play that song soon. We can't go through a school dance without hearing Ne-Yo," I reply. "Just chill. Maybe you can ask someone to dance."

Kevin stares at me like I'm speaking Japanese. "Gia, will you dance with me?" he asks.

"Okay, Kevin, but you better not step on my feet."

Ricky says, "So, I'll just stand over here on the side and look like a lame."

"It's only for a few minutes, Ricky. We'll be right back," I say.

Kevin pulls me by the wrist to the edge of the dance floor. It's a fast song with a reggae beat. Not a song that someone with two left feet would choose. But it's cool. As long as he just moves from side to side, he's cool.

"Gia," Kevin says over the music, "if you like Ricky, I understand. I won't be angry about it."

Why is everyone giving me permission to like Ricky just because he gave me a bracelet? I wish he had done that privately. This whole permission thing is getting old.

"Kevin . . . I don't want to think about liking anybody at this point. Just shut up and dance, please."

He smiles. "Okay, Gia. Whatever you say!"

I think I see a glimmer of wishful thinking in Kevin's eyes. This is too complicated for me. All of this who-likes-who stuff is, well, it makes me tired. I like things the way they were before hormones got all involved.

Kevin and I dance for the entire song, and then the DJ spins a slow cut. I'm ready to walk back over to Ricky until I notice that Kevin's hands are outstretched. Does he seriously want to attempt to slow dance with me?

Okay, in what world would I ever want Kevin to be my first slow dance?

But it's cool, because above everything else, Kevin is my homeboy. I won't count this as a real slow dance. I will count it as a practice. I'm pretty creative about how I count stuff . . . and I don't care what *you* think!

I'm so glad when the song is over. It's just painful. No . . . literally . . . painful, because Kevin has mashed every one of my toes.

And yes . . . I just said "mashed," like Mother Cranford.

Romeo slides up on the side of Kevin and me and says, "You wanna dance, lil' shorty?"

He already knows that I don't want to dance with him.

I don't even know what possessed him to ask. "No thanks, Romeo."

"You gonna hold that little grudge forever, lil' mama? Romeo is all about forgiving and forgetting," he replies.

"Seriously? Well, Gia is all about keeping it moving when someone plays Gia. Especially when the someone is named Romeo."

"Suit yourself, shorty. Dance with a lame if you want."

"Kevin's not a lame," I say in Kev's defense.

"It's cool, Gia. You don't have to argue over me," Kevin says. "I don't get mad about stuff that's not even true."

"Still, Kevin. He has no right to call you names."

Romeo laughs. "Gia, you shouldn't associate with lames. That makes people just think you're a lame too."

"So will people assume that I'm illiterate if I hang out with you?"

Before Romeo has a chance to answer, Ne-Yo blares out from the speakers. Ricky jogs across the floor and grabs my arm. "Come on, Gia! Kev, you know what to do!"

Ricky and I start our fluid dance step, and can I say that it is *hot*? This is the first time we've actually tried some real video choreography, but we've adapted it to our dance style.

It is completely awesome.

Then it really, really hits me. I'm always in perfect sync with Ricky. Not just with dancing but with everything. The only time we've ever even had anything close to an argument was when I was trying to kick it with Romeo.

It *has* always been me and Ricky. Everything about him is perfect. He's completely handsome and not conceited, because he doesn't even know how hot he is. And he actually cares about my feelings too. He's so perfect for me.

But, what if we do this whole dating thing and it's horrible? What if someone gets hurt . . . mainly me? What if someone's heart gets broken?

That would be all bad.

Kevin is doing his job as our "hyper man." He's got everyone saying, "Go, Ricky! Go, Gia!"

That's completely hot! I love hearing the crowd screaming my name. And I definitely like hearing it in the same sentence with Ricky's name.

Yeah, that sounds awesome . . . Ricky and Gia.

That's hot like fiyah!

IT IS
WHAT IT IS

Nikki Carter

ABOUT THIS GUIDE

The following questions are intended to
enhance your group's reading of
IT IS WHAT IT IS.

Discussion Questions

1. Should Gia feel happy about having a new step-sister? How would you feel if you were in Gia's shoes?

2. What do you think about Candy's shoplifting? Do you think it's a big deal? Would you have told on Candy?

3. What do you think of how Gia dealt with both her friends digging Ricky? Would you have handled it differently?

4. Why do you think Valerie didn't win the Home-coming Queen title? Would you vote for her?

5. It was totally cool of Gia to reach out and invite Valerie to go to the Homecoming dance with her crew. Have you ever been really kind to someone who's not a nice person? How did it make you feel?

6. What do you think of Kevin's semi-makeover? Does he have potential? Would you holla at him?

7. Do Gia and Ricky make a perfect couple? Why or why not? Do you think it would ruin their friendship if they became a couple?

8. What do you think is next for Gia's crew?

A Discussion with the Author

1. **Coke or Pepsi?**
Pepsi.

2. **What are your favorite TV Shows?**
Friday Night Lights, Smallville, Grey's Anatomy, and *Heroes* (Save the cheerleader, save the world!!! Yeah!).

3. **Bath or shower?**
Both.

4. **What's your most embarrassing moment?**
I was at a house party in my good friend's basement. I went upstairs to get a snack and when I headed back downstairs, I slipped and fell down the flight of stairs. The music stopped, but I just hopped up and started dancing. Trust . . . it was ALL bad!

5. **Who's your favorite actress?**
Sanaa Lathan! *Love and Basketball* is one of my favorite movies!

6. **Who's your favorite actor?**
I have more than one. Johnny Depp, Denzel Washington, and Idris Elba!

7. **Who's your favorite singer?**
This changes a lot. Right now, I'm feeling Beyoncé, Alicia Keys, and Jennifer Hudson. I also like fun gospel artists like KiKi Sheard.

8. **Have you ever been in love?**
Yes!

9. **If you could be a celeb for a day, who would you be?**
Hmm . . . Kimora Lee! She is running thangs. So fabulous!

10. **Flip-flops or Crocs?**
Umm . . . neither.

11. **What should readers learn from the So For Real series?**
The lesson is that it's okay to be unique and fearless! You can be a Christian and fab. Also, the people who appreciate you for doing YOU are the ones that you want in your life!

Want More?
Check out
IT'S ALL GOOD
by Nikki Carter.
Available in November 2009
wherever books are sold.

The answer is *no, ma'am*. Actually, the answer is a big, fat *no, ma'am*. There is no way I'm going to say yes to this foolishness, no matter how much my mother, Gwen, begs. No matter how much my Aunt Elena gives me that puppy dog stare.

The answer is no, and that's final.

What is the question, you ask? Well, Aunt Elena has a big idea. She calls it a big idea, and it's big all right. A big fat hot mess. But since she's the pastor's wife, everyone, including my mother, is going to back her up.

Aunt Elena wants to start purity classes at our church and she wants me to recruit girls to be a part of them. And not just girls from our church, but girls at school too. How about she just ask me to make a sign that says LAME and stick it on my forehead?

Of course, I'm down for being a member of the purity class. Because the flyness that is Gia Stokes is also the purest of pure. But I don't have any plans to go around the school announcing my virginity! That would be social suicide.

So I'm sitting here on my mother's favorite couch with my arms folded and a fierce frown on my face, while Gwen and Elena try their best to tag-team me.

"Gia, you are a youth leader! The younger girls look up to you," Elena says.

"She's right, Gia," Gwen agrees. "You would be good at this."

"Did anyone ask Hope to do this?" I ask.

I pose this question because Hope is the obvious choice. It would make sense, seeing that she is the pastor's daughter. Shouldn't she be required to endure the embarrassment of being part of the pastor's immediate family? She certainly gets to enjoy the perks!

"I did ask Hope, but she didn't want to do it," Elena replies.

I look to my mother for help. "So she gets to refuse, but I don't?"

Gwen says to Elena, "You neglected to mention that you asked Hope and she said no. I thought the two of them were going to work together."

Elena laughs. "You can't expect Hope to do something like this. She's not really cut out for it. It would come across better from Gia. She's more studious."

So my aunt is pretty much calling me a lame. And lames are supposed to be virgins, right? If I close my eyes tightly and concentrate really, really hard, will I be able to stop time and escape this madness?

"Are boys going to be in the classes too?" Gwen asks.

Aunt Elena laughs. "Of course not. This purity class will culminate in a debutante ball. I've never heard of a boy debutante."

"Well, boys should learn about purity too," my mother argues.

"That will have to be something for the men to address."

You've got to be kidding me! So, not only are we going to have a purity class (which I'm sure will be uncomfortable and embarrassing) but they're going to parade us around in poofy white dresses to prove that we graduated.

Good grief.

How about we talk about the reason my aunt came up with this ridiculous idea to begin with? This all started when my cousin Hope decided that she was going to go stark, raving boy crazy. Now Aunt Elena is all twisted, thinking that her precious daughter is going to be a teen pregnancy statistic or something. Hence, purity classes.

Hope pretty much flipped her wig at the beginning of the school year when she chose my best friend Ricky as her first big crush. She and Valerie, my co-captain on the Hi-Steppers, both competed for Ricky's affection. It was utterly ridiculous.

And, holla! He didn't pick either of them. I think he actually picked me! I say that I *think* he picked me because we haven't worked out all of the details on that. But, on the night of the Homecoming dance, he gave me a Tweety charm bracelet.

And that was totally something.

Clearly it was something because you don't just buy your best friend jewelry and it's nothing. Especially when that best friend is the perfect choice as a girlfriend! But it's been two weeks since Homecoming and there have been no can-I-be-your-boyfriend follow-up activities. Not a note, not a wink, nothing! Not even one of those distressed "I hate that I like you" looks, like that teen vampire on *Twilight*.

Nada. Zilch.

Gwen says, "I think that both Gia and Hope should recruit girls for the purity class. Y'all need to start with that fast-tailed Valerie."

Can you tell that Gwen no likee Miss Valerie? My mother has had beef with Valerie since she gave me a makeover when I was in the tenth grade. She also helped me sneak out on a date and other assorted foolishness. So yeah, Gwen has her reasons.

I want to remind Gwen of what Jesus would do in this scenario, but I also want to continue breathing so I decide against it.

"Mom, Valerie will not want to be in the purity class. Plus, I don't know if she qualifies. Do you have to be a virgin to be in it?"

Because if the answer is yes, Valerie is sooo not on the recruit list. I mean, I don't think she qualifies as an actual skank or anything, but she's pretty close. We're talking major nonvirginal activities.

"Absolutely!" says Elena. "The whole point of the class is to encourage young ladies who haven't taken that step yet."

I almost laugh out loud. Unfortunately, I think Hope and I are gonna have a hard time finding anyone in the junior class who will qualify. Maybe we'll start with the freshmen.

"Okay, Aunt Elena. I'll pass out a few flyers, but I'm not making any promises."

Elena kisses my cheek. "Thank you, sweetie!"

"But only if Hope has to help!" I add.

"Oh, all right," Aunt Elena says. "I'll tell Hope that she needs to assist you."

Gwen says, "Candy will help too. All three of you should be a great team."

I groan loudly. Candy is my all-around irritating step-sister. I spend enough of my downtime with her as it is, seeing that she macked her way onto the Hi-Steppers squad. Now I have to take purity classes with her too! So not the bidness.

My phone buzzes at my hip, taking my attention away from Gwen and Aunt Elena.

I read the text message from Ricky. **Hey You!**

See, this is what I'm talking about. What exactly does *hey you* even mean? Is that a greeting for a homegirl, or for someone you're trying to holla at? I think Ricky is purposely being ambiguous (go find your dictionary, boo) so that he doesn't have to deal with the possibility of *us*.

Since I don't know if I want to deal with that either, I understand his pain. But I'm going to need him to snap out of it and declare what the whole mystery of the Tweety bracelet means.

The Tweety bracelet that I've been rocking every day, like my *boyfriend* gave it to me!

I text Ricky back with an equally ambiguous: ☺

Take that, Ricky Ricardo.

"Who are you texting?" Gwen asks.

Mmm . . . kay. Why is Gwen all up in my bidness? "Ricky."

Gwen narrows her eyes and shares a glance with Aunt Elena. "Good grief. You girls are going to ruin Ricky with all of this attention."

"I agree. He's not the only boy on the planet," Aunt Elena adds.

"Uh, I'm only responding to a text that my friend sent me. You two are completely out of control."

Why is it that when I'm finally getting my little shine on, everybody wants to throw powder on it? Nobody, especially Aunt Elena, had any problem with Hope's desperate chasing of Ricky! Did anyone tell Hope to pump her brakes when she was writing him twenty-page letters?

The answer is no.

Did anyone tell Hope to stay home when Ricky made it abundantly clear that he was not trying to be her date for the Homecoming dance?

Yeah . . . that would be another no.

So they can absolutely save the hateration. They can save it for some time in the hopefully not-too-distant future, when Ricky is actually my boo.

Oooh, hold up a second. I'm going to have to give myself a lame citation for using the early-2000 term, "my boo." Womp, womp on me!

Gwen sighs and says, "We are not out of control. You young ladies are out of control, which is exactly why I'm one hundred percent for this purity class. All this boy chasing and carrying on must cease."

Did I just roll my eyes extra hard? Yeah, I totally did.

"I agree, Gwen. It's time we put our feet down and stop this madness!"

Okay, seriously, Auntie Elena is moving her mouth and sound is coming out, but she's not making one bit of sense.

"I said I'd be on your recruitment squad! Can I please be dismissed? You two don't need me in the room to discuss the state of today's teenager!"

Gwen narrows her eyes and turns to Aunt Elena. "Do you see what I have to deal with?"

"Hope isn't any better," Aunt Elena replies.

A growl escapes my lips as I storm off to my bedroom. I plop down on my brand-new, shiny Tweety comforter and pull my phone out. It's buzzing again.

Hi-Steppers meeting in two hours at IHOP.

This time it's Valerie blowing up my phone. I already know what she wants to meet about. The Longfellow Spartans are going to the state championship, and we have to do an extra-special routine.

Valerie should be glad she's still on the squad after what she pulled at the Homecoming game! She was extra-heated that she didn't win the Homecoming queen title and took over the halftime show. She had the drum major in the marching band give a speech about her and everything.

It was bananas!

Somehow, I think Valerie still isn't over that loss to quiet little Susan Chiang. She blames every single last person on the rally girls spirit squad, my cousin Hope included, for her not getting that Homecoming queen crown.

And if she's not over it . . . then the war is not over.

If I was one of the rally girls, I'd be taking cover. They're going to be walking down the hallway and out of nowhere, someone's going to yell, "Man down!" just like Keyshia Cole's mama on that reality show.

And trust . . . it's going to be *all bad*.

Gia's Playlist

Gia's got a soundtrack playing in her mind at all times! You can rock with Gia by listening to some of her favorite tracks.

Name	Artist
★ Sandcastle Disco	Solange
★ For Diva	Beyoncé
★ Good in the Hood	Tye Tribbett
★ Halo	Beyoncé
★ Take a Bow	Rihanna
★ Beautiful Girls	Sean Kingston
★ Need U Bad	Jazmine Sullivan
★ Lip Gloss	Lil' Mama